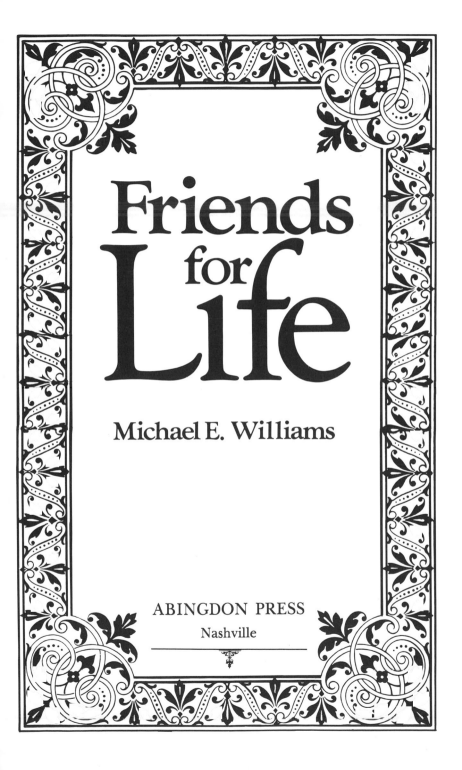

Friends for Life

Michael E. Williams

ABINGDON PRESS

Nashville

Friends for Life: A Treasury of Stories for Worship and Other Gatherings

Copyright © 1989 by Abingdon Press

Third Printing 1990

This book is printed on acid-free paper.

Library of Congress Cataloging-in-Publication Data

Williams, Michael E. (Michael Edward), 1950-
    Friends for life.

    Includes index.
    1. Bible stories, English. 2. Christian
fiction. 3. Friendship—Fiction. I. Title.
BS550.2.W55 1989   242   88-34401
ISBN 0-687-13516-8 (alk. paper)

Scripture quotations are from the Revised Standard Version of the Bible, copyright 1946, 1952, 1971 by the Division of Christian Education of the National Council of Churches of Christ in the U.S.A.

The four Christmas legends on pp. 79-84 are reprinted from "Tell Me a Christmas Story," *Christian Home* (Winter 1985–1986). Used by permission of The Upper Room.

MANUFACTURED IN THE UNITED STATES OF AMERICA

*This collection of stories is dedicated to
the people of*

First United Methodist Church,

*Columbia, Tennessee,
to whom many of them were first told,
and especially
for*

Margaret

Acknowledgments

Any collection of stories from the oral tradition depends on many storytellers. The more ancient stories in this volume were shaped by the voices and imaginations of many generations, before they came to me. For all those ancient and modern storytellers, whose names we no longer remember, I am grateful.

To my great-aunt, Minerva Cherry, from whom I first remember hearing stories, I offer unbounded appreciation for introducing me to the joys of the imagination, as well as for giving me a sense of belonging to a family and tradition. To my parents, John and Freda Willliams, for their gifts too numerous to list, including telling and reading me stories, I offer thanks.

The editors at Abingdon have been patient and conscientious companions on the journey toward transforming the spoken word into written text. Don Hardy, Chet Custer, Bob Conn, and Greg Michael have each made a unique contribution to the work that follows. The careful copy editing of Becky Marnhout helped guide my erratic spelling and punctuation and my eccentric phrasing toward greater clarity and precision.

If there are strengths in this collection of stories, many are due to the persons named above. They are not, however, to be blamed for its weaknesses. A saying from the African story tradition expresses it well: "If the story is beautiful, its beauty belongs to us all. If the story is not, the fault is mine alone who told it."

Contents

Introduction

In a letter she called her spiritual autobiography, Simone Weil wrote, "For nothing among human things has such power to keep our gaze fixed ever more intensely upon God, than friendship for the friends of God."[1] The friends of God are not only those whom we have encountered on the journeys of our lives. Their number also includes those persons from the Bible and Christian history whose lives we have shared through hearing their stories.

Here I have collected fifty-two stories, one for every Sunday in the year, all of them about the friends of God who have come to enrich my life. These stories are gathered into four clusters of a baker's dozen each: "Friends from the Hebrew Scriptures," "Friends from the Greek Scriptures," "Friends from Many Times," and "Friends from Many Places."

These stories are for reading. But they are not *only* for reading—they are for *telling*, too. I suggest that you not try to tell these stories word for word. Let the way I have written the story lead your own imagination to the way you will tell the story. Read more about the character portrayed and about those persons who were part of that character's life. This process of claiming the story as yours will give it a ring of authenticity that simply copying my telling will never give it.

---

1. George A. Panichas, ed., *The Simone Weil Reader* (New York: Daniel McKay, 1977), p. 19.

These stories are for worship. But they are not *only* for worship—they can be told *anytime*. They were first told as part of the services of worship in a local church. If your church has a time set aside for children during the worship service, you may wish to tell them there. If you are a pastor, you may wish to include one or more as a part of your sermon on Sunday. If you are a church school teacher, you might choose to include one in a lesson. If you are a parent, you may wish to share one of these stories with your children at bedtime, mealtime, or another time you have set aside for family devotions or stories.

These stories are for children. But they are not *only* for children—they are for *everyone*. Many of us suffer from the misunderstanding that stories are just for children, that we grow out of the need to hear them. Nothing could be further from the truth. Many adults have not met the friends of God whose stories are told here. Certainly you may wish to tell a story differently to preschool children than to adults, but people of all ages will enter into stories at the level at which they can best understand them.

I have collected these stories with the understanding that the persons told of here can become friends for life. Once you encounter them, they will live in your imagination for the rest of your days. In addition, they will enrich your life by their witness and offer options for living faithfully in the world of tomorrow.

If, as Simone Weil suggests, the best way to cultivate our relationship with God is to become friends of the friends of God, then their stories are their gifts to us. We are never too young to receive such gifts, nor too old to appreciate them. It is my hope that these stories will recall for their hearers some old friends and introduce some new ones, and that those who hear will know themselves as friends of God.

I

Friends from
the Hebrew Scriptures

Abraham was called "friend of God," but he was certainly not God's only friend. The Hebrew Scriptures are full of people who could be called friends of God: Sarah, David, Ruth, Naomi, Boaz—even a donkey. The Scriptures tell the stories of their friendships with each other and with God.

These stories were told in some cases for centuries before they were written down. Though later generations never knew these characters in the flesh, they came to know them as they heard their stories being told. Those later generations came to know that they were part of the same family as these ancient friends of God.

We are part of that same family. Abraham and Sarah are our ancestors, Ruth is our daughter-in-law, and Boaz is our cousin. Their stories welcome us as part of the family. We are a family that shares stories. We are a family that shares friendship with our Jewish and Islamic brothers and sisters, who know and love these stories as well. Perhaps most importantly, as we come to know the people of these stories and others of different traditions who love them, we grow in our friendship with the friends of God.

The Bible stories included in this section and the next are not simply rewordings of the texts from which they come. Rather, they are retellings of the stories. They attempt to re-create that event of the first telling/hearing of the story by weaving historical and cultural information into the telling. Many of the assumptions of that first group of hearers we no longer bring to the story in our time. Such information can be found in a number of Bible dictionaries and books on Bible life and times.

These retellings do not play fast and loose with the stories, however, nor do I suggest that you do so. While there is no one "right" way to tell a story, that doesn't mean we can tell them just any way we want.

It is my hope that these retellings honor the stories, their original tellers and hearers, and you.

1

Struggling with God

Genesis 18:16-33
God and Abraham

Too often, religious people seem to be judging others and calling down punishment on them. In this story Abraham defends before God those who don't deserve it. Perhaps a friend of God is a friend of people as well.

God knew of two cities where the people did terrible things to each other. It almost seemed that no one in them cared what was right or just, but only considered themselves. In thinking the whole matter through, God asked, "Am I going to tell Abraham about this situation, or am I going to have to make this decision all by myself?"

God had already promised that the descendants of Sarah and Abraham would be blessed so that they might be a blessing to all people. So God decided to tell Abraham what was planned for the inhabitants of Sodom and Gomorrah.

"Abraham," God began, "I have heard reports of the way the people of Sodom and Gomorrah treat each other, and I have decided to go see for myself if what I have heard is true. If it is, then the people there don't deserve to live."

Abraham spoke up almost without thinking: "Would you

13

really do away with the good as well as the bad? What if you found fifty people who were basically good folks? Remember, now, it really wouldn't do for you to make the good folks suffer along with the bad. Would the Judge of the world act unjustly? Would you save the cities for the sake of fifty good folks?"

"If I find fifty good folks, everyone shall escape punishment because of them," God answered.

Abraham spoke a second time. "Now, I am no one to be questioning you, nothing but dust and ashes. But what if you found forty-five good folks?"

"For the sake of forty-five, all will escape."

"How about forty?" Abraham was bargaining like a merchant.

"Fine, for forty."

"Now, don't get angry with me, but what about thirty?" Abraham was beginning to be somewhat cautious, not wanting to push God too far.

"Very well, for thirty," God's answer came.

"Now, I don't want to push too hard on this matter, but if you found twenty good people, would you save everybody?"

"For the sake of twenty, all will be saved."

Abraham knew he was reaching the end of his bargaining with God. But perhaps just once more . . . "I hope this doesn't irritate you, but if I could speak just once more . . . If you find as many as ten good folks?" Abraham's very tone of voice questioned whether he had gone too far.

"For the sake of as few as ten, I will not destroy even one." God's tone of voice said that this was the end of the matter. And so God left that place and Abraham to see if what had been said of the two cities was true—and to see if ten good folks could be found to save them.

That is the way Abraham bargained with God for the sake of Sodom and Gomorrah, for the good and bad alike.

Genesis 32:22-32

Jacob, the Wrestler, and Esau

Jacob is not the sort of character we admire, but like most tricksters, he holds a fascination for us. It seems he held a fascination for God as well.

Jacob was returning to meet his brother, Esau. The two had not met for many years. Jacob had cheated his brother out of his birthright and his blessing and had had to leave his home in fear for his life.

But that was years before, and Jacob had been through a great deal since them. He had been tricked by his uncle, Laban, and in turn took advantage of Laban's family when he had the chance. Now he was coming home, and he was afraid. Jacob knew that Esau was coming to meet him with a large number of men.

The evening before he would meet Esau, Jacob walked down by the Jabbok River. That night he met "someone," and they wrestled through the night. When it was almost time for the sun to rise, the Wrestler grabbed Jacob at the hip joint and threw his hip out of joint. But Jacob held on to his opponent.

"Let me go!" the Wrestler said. "Soon the sun will rise."

But Jacob held on tight and told his opponent, "I won't let you go until you bless me."

"What is your name?" was the Wrestler's only reply.

Jacob told his opponent his name.

"From now on you will have a new name. You will be called Israel because you have wrestled with God and God's people and won," the Wrestler told Jacob.

Jacob, now Israel, held on and said, "Tell me your name."

But the Wrestler would not, saying, "What is it to you what my name is?"

Then the Wrestler blessed Israel and was gone. Jacob limped to his camp and saw in the distance his brother, Esau.

When the two met there were no hard words. Esau embraced his brother and asked to meet his family. Jacob had gathered much of what he owned to give to Esau as a peace offering. But Esau would not accept it. "I have more than I need" was Esau's only answer.

The brothers who had begun life as enemies had after a long time become friends.

I have told these stories about two of my favorite characters from Genesis on numerous occasions. Each story could easily stand alone during a children's time in worship or be incorporated into a sermon or church school lesson. Both stories are about struggling with God. Abraham bargains with God to save the cities of Sodom and Gomorrah. Notice that Abraham does not condemn the cities just because God is prepared to. Rather, he takes their part in a conversation with God that sounds like it should be taking place between a merchant and a buyer in the marketplace. How many religious leaders today are ready to confront God in defense of the people when they are wrong, rather than speaking an additional word of condemnation? Moses would defend before God the lives (but not the actions) of his people when they built the golden calf. Perhaps the true sign of being God's chosen is a willingness to struggle with God for the sake of the people.

Jacob, on the other hand, is clearly a rascal, which may be one reason he remains such an interesting character. Because he is willing to take advantage of his situation with the Wrestler, just as he has taken advantage of every other situation in the story, he gains a blessing and a new name. The new name, Israel, means "I have wrestled with God and God's people and won." How would you like to carry a name like that through life?

Remember, Jacob limped away from that river bank on the leg that was wounded in the struggle. Both blessed and wounded, he goes to meet his brother Esau.

For other stories about these two, see the following:

Genesis 12:1-9   Abram's and Sarai's call
Genesis 15:1-21   God's covenant with Abram and Sarai

Genesis 16:1-16   *The conflict between Sarah and Hagar*
Genesis 18:1-15   *Sarah's laughter*
Genesis 21:1-7   *The birth of Isaac, child of laughter*
Genesis 22:1-19   *The near-sacrifice of Isaac*
Genesis 27:1–28:5   *Jacob cheats Esau*
Genesis 29:1-30   *Jacob marries Leah and Rachel*

2

Joseph and His Brothers

Genesis 37:1-36
Joseph and His Brothers, I

Do you know anyone who is the teacher's pet or the favored child in a family? How do you feel toward him or her? How do you think you would feel if Joseph were your brother?

Joseph was the favorite son of Jacob. While his brothers wore the rough tunics of shepherds, Jacob gave Joseph a beautifully decorated robe with long sleeves. Only one who never had to do hard work could wear long sleeves. Jacob never hesitated to show that Joseph was his favorite, and as a result Joseph grew to be a spoiled brat.

When he could be talked into helping his brothers with the sheep, he brought back stories to his father telling everything his brothers had done wrong. Even at seventeen, long after even the most spoiled youngster had grown out of it, Joseph remained a tattletale.

It seemed that the more his father loved Joseph, favoring him and overlooking his self-centeredness, the more his brothers hated him.

To make things worse, Joseph began to have dreams. If he had kept them to himself, it would not have been so bad. But he told them to his brothers. One day he came to his brothers and said, "Listen to this dream I had. We were all out working together. We were tying sheaves of grain together and stacking them in the field. Suddenly, my sheaf of grain stood up, and all of yours bowed down to it. What do you suppose that means?"

"All he ever does is dream about work. He certainly never did any," one brother said with scorn.

"Do you mean that you, Daddy's boy, are going to be ruler over us?" It would have been funny if it hadn't made his brothers angrier than ever at him.

A short time later, he told them another dream. "In this one," he said, "the sun and moon and eleven stars all bowed down to me."

This was just too much. Joseph's brothers went to Jacob and told him what his pampering of the boy had led to. Jacob called his favorite son in and asked him, "What is this dream you told your brothers? Are your mother and your brothers and I all to bow down to you?" But Joseph made no answer.

Jacob thought about the worsening situation in his family, while the brothers became even more jealous of Joseph.

One day later Jacob sent Joseph to see about his brothers, who were keeping sheep near a place called Shechem. But his brothers had moved their flocks to other grazing lands near Dothan. Since Joseph had no idea where his brothers were or how to find them, he simply wandered through the fields near Shechem until someone found him and pointed him in the direction his brothers had gone.

As he approached their camp, Joseph's brothers saw him coming and said, "Look, here comes the boy who is full of dreams." They also saw their chance to get rid of him. Some wanted to kill him, but Reuben suggested they throw him into one of the dry cisterns nearby.

When Joseph arrived the brothers took him, stripped him of his beautiful robe, and threw him into an empty cistern. Now, it had been Reuben's plan to come back, retrieve Joseph from the cistern, and take him back to Jacob. But while Reuben was away, a caravan of traders passed by, carrying goods to Egypt. The brothers pulled Joseph from the cistern and sold him to the traders.

When Reuben found out what had happened, he asked what they would tell their father. They finally decided to dip Joseph's robe in the blood of a goat and take it to their father, leading him to believe that the boy had been killed by a wild animal.

When they returned to Jacob and showed him the robe, they told him, "Here, we found this. Is this your son's robe?"

When Jacob saw the robe, he tore his own clothes and cried aloud, "My son has been torn to pieces by an animal!" Then he wept and mourned for his son, and none of his other children could comfort him.

As Jacob mourned, Joseph was taken by the traders to Egypt and sold there as a slave.

Genesis 45:4-15

Joseph and His Brothers, II

Have you ever met anyone you just didn't like from the start, yet who later became a friend? We often misjudge people by dwelling on our first impressions of them. What do you think of Joseph in this story?

There was a terrible famine in the land where Joseph's father and brothers lived. Joseph had not lived there since being sold into slavery many years before. He had served as a slave and lived through a time in prison, to become second only to Pharaoh in authority and power. He now had an Egyptian name, an Egyptian wife and family, and lived as a wealthy Egyptian prince.

Joseph had gained his position by interpreting Pharaoh's dreams of the years of plenty and famine. He then had stored enough food for the people of Egypt and many more. When the years of famine came, people arrived at his court every day, asking Joseph for food.

Among those who came for food were Joseph's brothers. They did not recognize him because he looked and talked and acted like an Egyptian now. But he recognized them. At first he accused them of being spies. He only allowed the brothers to return home after he had exacted from them the promise to bring their youngest brother Benjamin with them if they ever returned. He sent them home with bags of grain, in which he had placed the bags of money with which they had paid for the food. When they discovered this, his brothers were afraid that the powerful Egyptian might think they had stolen the money.

After a time the grain they bought ran out, and the brothers had to return to Egypt. On their return they would have to bring their youngest brother, Benjamin, with them. Jacob did not want Benjamin to leave, but after the brothers promised his son's safe return, their father agreed.

This time, when they arrived at Joseph's, they offered him twice the amount of money they had found in their bags after the last visit, but Joseph told them their God must have put it there, for he had been paid. Then he invited the brothers to eat at his table. After a large and elegant meal the brothers slept. As they did, Joseph had a servant place a silver cup in Benjamin's bag of grain.

After the brothers started for home, they were stopped and accused of taking something from the house of Joseph. When all the bags were searched, Joseph's cup was found in Benjamin's bag. When they were returned to Joseph's presence, he told his brothers that Benjamin would have to remain in Egypt.

When he heard this, Judah begged Joseph, "Please, keep me here instead of my brother. It would kill our father to lose his youngest. You see, he already lost the son he loved the most. If he lost another, he would surely die."

Hearing the love Judah had for their father, Joseph could no longer restrain himself. He sent everyone else from the room and told his brothers whom they had been dealing with. "I am Joseph, your brother. God has used me to bring you to a new land and a new life. Do not feel ashamed or angry with yourselves because of what you did to me years ago. You meant it to do me harm, but God meant it to do good for me and for you."

So Joseph sent his brothers back to their home to get their father and bring the entire family to live in Egypt, in a land called Goshen. This is where their descendants lived until the time of Moses.

I usually tell the stories of Joseph as a mini-series. Each episode leaves Joseph in a difficult situation, and I tell my listeners that they will just have to come back to hear how he will get out of it. The appeal of this story is certainly not limited to Sunday morning. It could be told during a series of evening programs for youth, since some of the subject matter is a bit mature for children.

These episodes could provide the model for a series of sermons on characters in the longer story. Prepare each story in your own words, just as I have done here. For deeper insight into these stories, attempt to tell an episode from another character's point of view, for example, that of Joseph's father or Potiphar's wife or Pharaoh's chief cupbearer who forgot Joseph for so long. (This is a good tip for deepening the experience of any story.)

Other stories about Joseph include these:

Genesis 39:1-20	*Joseph in Potiphar's house*
Genesis 39:21–40:23	*Joseph in prison*
Genesis 41:1-39	*Joseph interprets Pharaoh's dreams*

3

The Birth of Moses

Exodus 1:8-20
Shiphrah and Puah

The Bible's stories were not told to provide simple morals, like Aesop's fables. They are about real people struggling to know God in difficult and confusing situations. In this tale two Hebrew midwives make up a story to tell Pharaoh in order to save the lives of Hebrew children. What would you have done in their place?

In the ancient days before the Hebrew people came out of Egypt, many customs were different than in our time. For example, when it came time for a woman to deliver her child, she was placed on a birthstool. This birthstool may have been a circular stone (or possibly two stones) upon which the one about to give birth sat as she was assisted by one or more midwives.

The role of the midwife was to assist the mother in the birth and immediately upon the child's arrival to determine whether it was male or female. Then the midwife took charge of the child, cutting the cord that still attached it to its mother, washing it, and rubbing it with salt.

It is little wonder, then, that when a certain pharaoh wanted to harm the Hebrew people who had lived in Egypt for generations, he would call upon the midwives for help. It happened this way.

Long after the Hebrew, Joseph, had served as Pharaoh's steward, second in power only to the king of Egypt, there came to the throne a pharaoh who did not remember him. All he knew was that there were many Hebrews living in his land, and he considered them foreigners. This pharaoh began to stir up the hatred of the people against the Hebrews.

"What if the Hebrews were to outnumber us, and what if we went to war with another country, and what if the Hebrews decided that they liked our enemies better than they liked us, and what if they rose up against us? They could destroy everything we have worked so hard to create." And so Pharaoh caused his people to fear the Hebrews.

Now, by this time the Hebrews must have ceased to think of themselves as foreigners. After all, Joseph had been one of theirs. So they must have been terribly bewildered when they were set to work building cities for Pharaoh under the eyes and authority of Egyptian bosses. But they were loyal citizens and worked hard. The work seemed to agree with them, because the more difficult the tasks set before them, the more the Hebrew people thrived.

Which frightened Pharaoh even more. He made them work harder, hoping that building his cities would weaken the people instead of strengthening them. But just to ensure the doom of these foreigners, Pharaoh called upon two Hebrew midwives to help him. Their names were Shiphrah and Puah.

Pharaoh asked Shiphrah and Puah to continue to go about their duties helping the Hebrew women deliver their babies. Since the first thing they did following a birth was to see if the child was a girl or a boy, they were to do just that. But here Pharaoh's instructions became terrifying. He told the midwives if the child was female to continue to care for it as they usually did. But if the child was male, they were to take it from its mother, kill it, and tell her it had been born dead.

As they left, the hated instructions still echoing in their ears, Shiphrah and Puah both carried the same thought in their hearts. When they were far from Pharaoh's presence, they would speak it to each other. They would not do what they had been ordered to do. Pharaoh was a fearsome ruler, but they agreed that their God was more awesome still. They would not kill the male children of their people.

But Pharaoh would expect a report from them. What would they tell him? They decided to tell the same story. "These Hebrew women are strong, much stronger than the women of your people. By the time we arrive they have delivered their boys, have seen them, and know that they are healthy. What could we do under such circumstances?"

When they returned to Pharaoh and told him their story, it just made him more fearful. He just knew that these slaves were stronger than his people. After all, they had to be stronger; it was natural—they did the work. For the time being the midwives and the Hebrew sons were safe.

Because of their willingness to follow God rather than Pharaoh, the midwives Shiphrah and Puah were blessed with families of their own. At the same time the Hebrew people became stronger in numbers, as well as becoming even stronger workers. And Pharaoh became even more afraid of them.

The story of the Hebrew midwives might be told on an occasion when discussion would follow—in a youth or adult church school class, for example. The situation of the conflicting values of telling the truth or being accomplices in the death of children is as complex and full of feeling as real life. Because of that complexity, it might be good to set it beside similar modern dilemmas, or to ask class members to recall situations in their lives when they had a choice between two less than ideal paths.

For other stories about the children of Israel and Moses, see:

Exodus 3:1–4:17	*Moses and the burning bush*
Exodus 12:31-42	*The slaves leave Egypt*
Exodus 13:17-22	*Pillars of cloud and of fire lead the slaves*

Exodus 14:19-31	*Crossing the sea*
Exodus 32:1-24	*The golden calf and Moses' argument with God*
Exodus 33:12-23	*Moses views God's glory*
Deuteronomy 34:1-12	*The death of Moses*

4

Lifesavers

Numbers 22
Balaam and the Donkey

*Sometimes we think that God only cares for human beings or,
even worse, that God cares for only certain persons or groups.
Here is a story in which an animal can see more clearly than a
seer. God seems to like to turn the tables on us like that.*

Once when the children of Israel were journeying, they came
to camp in the land called Moab. The king of that area was
Balak, and he feared this new group of people. So he sent a
number of very important officials from his kingdom to a seer
named Balaam, asking him to come and curse the Israelites.

Balaam told the officials that they were to be his guests that
night and that he would have an answer for them in the morning.
Now, Balaam was not a Hebrew, but he knew and respected the
God the Hebrews worshiped. That night God told him not to go
with the company back to Balak. So the next morning he refused
to accompany them and sent them on their way with his answer
for Balak. No, he would not curse these people.

When Balak received the answer from Balaam, the king
assumed that he had not offered Balaam enough gold and
silver, or that his representatives had not been impressive
enough. So he sent the most important officials in his kingdom

with an even better offer to Balaam, asking him to curse the children of Israel.

Once again Balaam received the visitors and heard their request. But he made clear to them that all the silver and gold in Balak's house would not make him go against the commands of God. Again he asked them to spend the night, telling them they would have his answer in the morning. This time God told Balaam, "You will go with Balak's people, but you will do only what I tell you to do and say only the words I put in your mouth."

The next morning Balaam and the group started off to see Balak. Balaam was riding his donkey, and when they came to a narrow place in the road with the stone walls of vineyards on either side, the donkey saw an angel of God standing in the path, holding a sword. The donkey, being a sensible animal, turned aside and walked into a field. Balaam, who couldn't see the angel, thought the donkey was being stubborn and beat her with his stick. In this way the donkey saved Balaam's life.

A second time the donkey approached the angel standing between the two walls. Pushing too close to one of the walls, the donkey mashed Balaam's foot against it. The seer beat the donkey again. The donkey had protected Balaam a second time.

A third time the donkey was forced down the road where the angel stood, but this time she simply lay down in the middle of the road. Again Balaam took his stick to her. For a third time, Balaam's life was spared on account of his donkey.

Much to Balaam's surprise, the donkey began to speak: "Why do you beat me? Am I not your donkey, the one you have ridden every day since the time I came to live in your household? Have I ever done anything to harm you?"

Balaam, still angry, said, "If I had a sword I would kill you."

Then the angel spoke and told Balaam that the donkey had saved his life. If she had not stopped when she did, she would still be alive, but Balaam would not. "Continue on your journey," the angel told Balaam, "but say only the words God puts in your mouth."

So Balaam continued on to Balak's palace. Three times

preparations were made for Balaam to curse the children of Israel. But the seer remembered what the angel had said and spoke only the words that God put in his mouth. Instead of curses, three times Balaam blessed the Hebrews.

These blessings were remembered by the children of Israel as they journeyed on, long after the day when Balaam spoke them and departed from a very disappointed Balak.

Ruth
Naomi and Ruth

This strange love story between a mother-in-law and daughter-in-law, between Naomi from Bethlehem and the foreigner, Ruth, is one of the two most powerful stories of friendship in the Bible. What do we learn about God's friendship with us and our friendships with each other from such surprising relationships?

Naomi was a foreigner. She had come with her husband to Moab, where they had lived and raised two sons. Then the worst that could happen, did happen. Her husband and her two grown, married sons died, leaving her with two Moabite daughters-in-law on her hands.

Naomi heard that things were going well at Bethlehem, her family home in Judah, so she decided to return. Before returning, however, she called her daughters-in-law, Orpah and Ruth, together to tell them good-bye. Her farewell was really a blessing, wishing for the two young women a full and rich life in the future. At first, neither of her daughters-in-law wanted to part from this woman they loved.

Seeing that neither was going to leave, Naomi changed her tactics. How could she take foreigners home with her? She had no way to support even herself. She asked the young women, "Am I going to have sons at my age? Even if I could, would you wait for them to grow up, to have a family? Just because I have suffered misfortune is no reason that your lives should be as bitter as mine." The three women wept for each other and for themselves. Orpah kissed her mother-in-law as she left to return to her family. But Ruth refused to leave.

Instead, Ruth made this vow of friendship that has become familiar through many generations of repetition: "Entreat me not to leave you or to return from following you; for where you go I will go, and where you lodge I will lodge; your people shall be my people, and your God my God; where you die I will die, and there will I be buried. May the Lord do so to me and more also if even death parts me from you." That ended the matter, but not the story.

So Naomi and her Moabite daughter-in-law returned to Bethlehem. Ruth collected food for them by picking up the barley left behind by those who gathered landowners' crops. That was the way the poor were fed in those days, by gathering whatever they could from the leftovers in the fields. The particular fields from which Ruth gleaned belonged to Boaz, a relative of Naomi's.

Boaz took notice of the young Moabite woman and began to show her special favors. He knew of her deep love for Naomi and the kindness she had shown her mother-in-law. Boaz planned carefully to gain the right from other family members to marry Ruth. Naomi advised her daughter-in-law on her behavior toward this older male relative who had taken such an interest in her. Finally, Ruth and Boaz were married.

But her marriage seemed to strengthen the bond between Ruth and Naomi. Ruth had a son, and when Naomi showed him off to her friends, they told her, "How fortunate you are to have such a daughter-in-law; she is more to you than any number of sons." In those days, that was saying quite a lot. Ruth's son was named Obed, who in later years became the father of Jesse. Jesse, you may remember, was the father of David, the ancestor of Jesus.

This story was written by an unknown teller during a time when the men of Israel were being encouraged to divorce their foreign wives. The storyteller just wants to remind us that the wife of Boaz, the grandmother of David, was a foreigner from Moab. But before she was any of these, Ruth was a friend to Naomi.

I Samuel 18:1-4; 20:35-42; 23:16-18

David and Jonathan

This is the second important biblical story of friendship,
following that of Ruth and Naomi. David, the shepherd who
had been anointed king, and King Saul's son, Jonathan, who
his father and many others thought would be king, become
friends. Which do you think takes more courage and integrity,
to step up to the throne as David did, or to step back from the
throne for the sake of friendship, as did Jonathan?

If anyone had reason to distrust David, Jonathan surely did.
After all, Jonathan was the oldest son of King Saul and should
have expected to become king after his father. David was a
shepherd from Bethlehem who was anointed king by Samuel
while Saul was still king. The king was in a terribly troubled
state of mind when he brought David into the royal household
to play music he hoped would drive his terrors away. Little did
Saul realize that his troubles were only beginning.

Saul grew to hate David. After this shepherd boy killed the
giant, Goliath, who had frightened the king and all of his
soldiers, his name became a household word. David grew to be
a successful leader, drawing greater attention than Jonathan.
His victories in battle were celebrated more than the king's.
The people sang, "Saul has killed his thousands, and David his
tens of thousands." This angered the troubled king so greatly
that he set for David outlandishly unreasonable tasks, in the
hope that the young man would be killed. When David
returned unharmed from each one, having done more than
the king had asked, Saul's hatred grew into an obsession. He
regretted allowing this shepherd into his household and vowed
to rid the world permanently of David one way or another.
Several times in fits of anger Saul threw his spear at the young
musician as he played, barely missing him each time.

Through all his father's plotting against David, Jonathan saw
the young musician as a brother, not a threat. The people
celebrated David's victories, while Jonathan was hardly

noticed. Yet this never seemed to affect the friendship between the two young men. When they first came to know each other, Jonathan gave David his own robe and armor, to show his respect and as a sign of friendship.

One day Saul became so angry at David that he cried out to his son and his soldiers to kill the young man. But Jonathan's friendship was stronger than his father's anger. He ran to warn David of the king's desire to see him dead and urged him to hide until the fire of Saul's rage had died down. Back at his father's side, Jonathan tried to cool Saul's temper as he spoke of David's innocence, and he asked the king to spare the life of his friend. For a time David was able to return, but it was not long before Saul's fury lashed out stronger than ever.

This time Jonathan told David that he would plead once again with his father for his friend's life. The two agreed upon a signal that would tell David whether to return or escape. Jonathan would come to the place where David would be hiding and bring a servant with him. He would shoot an arrow. If he told the servant that the arrow had landed on "this side" of the place where David hid, it was safe for David to return. If, on the other hand, he told the servant that the arrow had landed on "the other side" of the hiding place, David was to flee for his life.

The next day was the feast of the new moon, a time when everyone was expected to dine with the king. When David did not appear, Saul asked where he was. Jonathan said he had gone home to Bethlehem to be with his family. The king flew into a rage and cursed his son, saying he had chosen that "son of Jesse" to his own shame. When Jonathan defended his friend, Saul threw a spear at his own son, as he had at David before, but the young man was able to escape unharmed.

Jonathan went to David's hiding place and shot the arrow beyond his servant, telling him loudly so David could hear that it had fallen on the "other side." Then he sent the servant home with his weapons. David came out of hiding to see his friend, and the two promised loyalty to each other, not only for themselves but for all their children and grandchildren and great-grandchildren, forever.

When the two friends met again, Jonathan told David that

both he and Saul realized that David would be king. Jonathan was content to be with the new king to help him as he ruled. Jonathan risked his father's respect, his very life, and gave up the possibility of being a king, for a friend. He truly loved David as he loved himself. Now that is a friend.

Sometimes we speak of our friends as lifesavers. These three stories are about the kind of friendship that literally saves lives. Balaam is saved by an animal, his faithful donkey, who sees more clearly than her rider. While this donkey is no Lassie or Rin Tin Tin, nearly any child or adult could identify with her loyalty, and by extension with the friendship of a pet that exceeds the care and concern of her human friend.

The friendship that grew up between the Hebrew Naomi and Ruth, her foreign daughter-in-law, is a model of a relationship that deepens throughout life. At first it seemed that Naomi only wanted to rid herself of her foreign daughters-in-law, but Ruth refused and returned with Naomi to her home. Then Ruth proceeded to save both from starvation by picking up the grain left behind when the barley fields of Boaz were harvested. With the clever assistance of Naomi, Ruth saved the family line by marrying Boaz and presenting Naomi with a grandson. The women of the village told Naomi, "Such a daughter-in-law is worth more than seven sons." In that time and place this represented the finest friendship anyone could imagine.

In the third story Jonathan saves the life of his friend David, though it is Saul, Jonathan's father, who wishes David dead. The two young men declare their lifelong friendship, which does last even after David becomes king—a position that Jonathan might well have hoped he would inherit.

Although these stories are suitable for any group, each presents a unique emphasis on friendship that makes it especially appropriate for these specific groups:

Balaam—children
Ruth—women's groups
David—men's groups

You may wish to follow each telling by asking your listeners to remember friends who have been lifesavers for them.

5

The Wisdom of the Wise

I Kings 3:5-13
Solomon and God

Solomon has been known throughout history for his wisdom. This brief story is like many others around the world. In it, Solomon is offered the chance to wish for anything in the world. If someone offered you the same chance, what would you choose?

Things had not always been well in David's family. There had been much unfriendliness and downright hatred between family members. Sometimes the king's heart was broken by the lack of love he saw there. Sometimes it was the king himself who was not very loving.

After David's death his son, Solomon, became king. One day he went to a high place to worship God. After Solomon worshiped he slept, and as he slept God's voice came to him. "Ask whatever you want; whatever it is, I will give it to you."

Solomon spoke in the dream: "You have shown kindness to my father David and to me. Now that I am king I feel like a child. You have made your servant a leader among your people. So I ask for a heart of understanding so that I might judge wisely, knowing what is right and what is wrong."

Again God spoke: "You have chosen well. You did not ask for a long life, you did not ask for riches, you did not ask to defeat your enemies. Rather, you have asked for a heart of understanding in order that you might act with justice for all the people.

"Since you have chosen the wisest course, I will add all the other good things of life to you. You will reign with wisdom and justice and be remembered by the people."

Solomon did rule long and well. He is remembered, and when his name is mentioned it is because he was someone who had a heart of understanding.

Proverbs 2:13-18
Wisdom and People

It is hard to become friends with a faceless idea or to love a concept. Whatever we would become friends with, we put a face on. The ancient teachers knew this. If we are to become friends of wisdom, we must be able to see it face to face. Listen in on this imagined conversation among several rabbis, as they talk about one of the faces of wisdom we read about in Proverbs.

The scholars sat in the house of study, speaking together of wisdom. "What shall we teach our children and all the generations to follow about wisdom?" they asked.

"Wisdom is much more than the gathering of facts like so many pretty stones," remarked one.

"Wisdom is more than showing off one's learning before others, as some of our teachers do," warned another.

"Which certainly doesn't apply to any of us here," laughed a third.

"We are very good at saying what wisdom is not," spoke a young scholar, "but which of us can paint wisdom's portrait?"

The oldest of the teachers there, who had not spoken yet,

stirred and said, "Wisdom must paint her own portrait, for she was the artist who stood at God's side as together they painted the universe into being. She was God's companion from before there was anything, and it was through her that creation became the beautiful and intricate mosaic that it is. When we look at the beauties of earth, sea, and sky, we can offer thanks to God and Lady Wisdom."

"Well spoken," replied another elder, "but I must say that when Wisdom speaks to me, which I admit is rarely, it is in the voice of my mother. She speaks out of love because she wants the very best life has to offer for me. At times she corrects me when I wander from the way. But she knows and I know that in sharing herself she offers her child a gift more precious than silver or gold."

"Why does Wisdom not respond to the urgent need to correct the injustices of our age?" A fire burned behind this speaker's eyes. "Wisdom is a woman running down the street, calling out to anyone who will listen. She is trying to get people to turn from their selfishness and hear a word that will keep them from destroying creation and each other. But do they listen? No! They make fun of her, and few are the hands that reach to her as she reaches out to us."

"On the other hand," said another, "I see Wisdom as a woman who built a house and furnished it with everything necessary for life. She invites whoever will to come and learn what is really important in life. In her house people stand in awe of God, who after all is the beginning of wisdom. Those who live in the house of Wisdom live for God and others."

The discussion continued late into the night. The scholars could only agree that while none had captured the whole beauty of wisdom, each had offered a glimpse. As they prepared to go to their homes, the oldest scholar spoke a word of benediction: "Wisdom is our friend, who invites us to journey with her. As we walk with her and learn all her ways, we come to know that 'all her ways are pleasantness and all her paths are peace.' "

These two stories about wisdom are different in several ways. First, one is about a male and the other a female.

Second, one is taken from the long narrative about the family of David, and the other is part of the collection of wisdom sayings we call Proverbs.

These two stories are not really for children but for those who have lived long enough to have learned how little they really know. They might be especially appropriate for students, faculty, or any community that places a high value on learning.

Another character you may wish to look up in this same tradition is Koheleth, the preacher in Ecclesiastes.

6

The Friendship of God

Job 42:1-6
Job, His Friends, and God

Does God punish those who do evil and reward those who do good? If something bad happens to someone, does that mean he or she has done wrong? Some people used to think so, until they heard the story of Job. What do you think?

Some friends Job had. He was a good person, and everyone knew it. He even said prayers for his children just in case they did something to offend God without realizing it. Then the bottom fell out. He lost everything—the family, the farm, his health.

Job found himself sitting on an ash heap scraping his sores with broken pottery, wondering what had gone wrong. Job's friends joined him, and for a while they were able to keep their mouths shut. When Job started to curse the day he was born, they decided it was time to explain to him his problem.

Friend 1: "Obviously, you did something wrong. If you hadn't done something, you wouldn't be suffering now."

Job: "I didn't do anything wrong, at least not anything worse than you. But I'm the one sitting here in the ashes of my life, scraping my sores while you hand out advice."

Friend 2: "Just say you're sorry for what you did, and maybe God will show you mercy."

Job: "I didn't do anything wrong, I'm telling you. Not to deserve this, I didn't. How can I say I'm sorry if I didn't do anything?"

Friend 3: "After all, you're just a human being and humans make mistakes. Just say you're sorry and get it over with."

Job: "Mistakes! Mistakes, you say. Does this look like the punishment for a mistake? People kill other people and don't suffer like this. I have lost everything I value—my family, my livelihood, my health. Now I think I'm losing my mind."

Friends: "Look, we are just trying to help. We're telling you the latest research to come out of the seminary guilt/punishment research project. But if you don't want to listen . . ."

Job: "I will listen, all right. I will listen when God arrives with evidence that I deserve what I'm suffering. I have kept my integrity this long, and I don't intend to give it up now. Not for friends like you."

The crazy thing is that God did arrive, and not a minute too soon. Job was about to send his friends packing. But when God arrived, God presented no evidence that Job deserved what he was suffering. There *was* no such evidence. We all knew that from the beginning of this story.

What God did do was ask Job a series of questions that no one could have answered, like where he was when the foundations of the world were laid, or was it his yardstick that measured the universe. Well, this went on for a while until Job figured that unless you were God, you were never going to figure out why he was suffering. But it certainly wasn't for the reason Job's so-called friends had suggested.

The whole event left Job speechless, except to say, "God, you know everything and I, uh, *we* don't know much of anything for sure. I spoke better than I knew, before, saying things too wonderful for me or anyone else to understand. Now that we have had this little talk, though, I am ready to turn and go in another direction."

God seemed satisfied with that, because the next thing you know Job's friends are all ordered by God to serve Job. Even if he didn't know what he was saying, Job held onto his integrity, which made more sense than anything his friends said.

Jeremiah 18:1-11
Jeremiah, the Potter, and God

Bible stories speak of God and our relationship to God by using many images. Jeremiah speaks of God as a potter who does not throw a pot away just because it doesn't turn out exactly right the first time. Are the friends of God continually being reshaped into new forms?

Jeremiah was a prophet who was never sure whether God was friendly or not. One morning Jeremiah woke up and heard God telling him to go to a potter's house and watch the potter at work. God seems to always be telling prophets to do strange things and saying that they will learn something important from the experience.

So Jeremiah went to watch the potter throw pots. At first he couldn't figure out why God had told him to take part in this educational activity. Then, as the potter raised one particular pot, his hand slipped and he made a mess of it. The prophet watched as the potter pounded the clay back into a lump and patiently began to shape another pot. It was then that Jeremiah realized that it was just this remaking of a pot that God wanted him to see.

After that, God said to the prophet, "Don't you think I am a lot like that potter? I can raise up people and nations just like the potter did. Sometimes they come out all wrong, just as you saw happen with the one pot. But when they do I don't just throw them away. No, I work them back into a lump and start all over again. And sometimes they turn out very differently than the first time."

Jeremiah warned the people that they might have to take a pounding to become a new people. What Jeremiah didn't realize at the time was that he would have to take a pounding in order to become a new prophet.

Both Job and Jeremiah came to know God's friendship, but both came to it the hard way.

Even when God's voice challenged Job out of the whirlwind, this man who had lost everything knew that God was more friend to him than those who had tried to explain his suffering to him.

Jeremiah found an image of God's friendship in a workplace, a potter's shop, in the relationship between the potter and the clay being formed into some useful vessel. This image of God's friendship did not make Jeremiah's calling as a prophet any easier, just more understandable.

These stories are suitable for anyone who has experienced or is experiencing hard times, such as persons in a grief or divorce recovery group. Yet since most of us have experienced hard times at some time in our lives, these images of God's friendship may just be for all of us.

7

Walking Through Fire

Daniel 3:1-30
Shadrach, Meshach, and Abednego

Sometimes we speak of suffering as "walking through the fire." The three young men in this story walk through the fire for their faith because they will not worship anyone or anything but God. Do you know of people who have suffered because they will not put their loyalty to a country, a political party, or even a church above their faith in God?

It was during the days when Nebuchadnezzar was king over Babylon, and Daniel, the Jewish assistant to the king was the king's administrator, that the following story was told. The king decided he wanted to create a statue ninety feet high and nine feet wide. That in itself was not so bad. Then he had the statue placed on the plain of Dura, which was not necessarily a problem either. Then Nebuchadnezzar called all of his bureaucrats together—his satraps, prefects, viceroys, counselors, judges, chief constables, and the governors of all his provinces. This was certainly not unusual.

When all the bureaucrats were gathered before the statue, the king's herald announced, "All you people of every language, race, or ethnic background, it is the king's command that when you hear the horn, pipe, zither, triangle, dulcimer, and music and singing of every kind, you are to throw yourselves on your faces and worship the statue that King Nebuchadnezzar has so graciously provided. And any of you who are thinking that you might not throw yourselves on your faces and worship the statue need to know that if you don't, you will be thrown into a fiery furnace."

Well, the herald didn't have to repeat that last part twice. As soon as the people heard the sound of the horn, pipe, zither, triangle, dulcimer, and music and singing of every kind, they threw themselves on their faces and worshiped the golden statue that King Nebuchadnezzar had so graciously provided.

Just about that time there was one group who got up off their faces and went to the king. They said, "Long live the king! Didn't we hear you say that everybody who hears the horn, pipe, zither . . ."

"That's right," said the king; "get on with it."

"Or else they will be thrown into a fiery furnace?"

"So?" The king was getting more than a little impatient.

"Well, there are three Jews named Shadrach, Meshach, and Abednego, whom you appointed to be bureaucrats just like us, who did not throw themselves on their faces and worship the statue that you have so graciously provided. We think they must be atheists."

Hearing this report, Nebuchadnezzar was very upset. After all, you can't have citizens falling down on their religious duties. So the king called Shadrach, Meshach, and Abednego to appear before him. When they appeared he asked them, "Is it correct what I hear about you boys being atheists?"

To which the three responded, "Don't be ridiculous. Of course it's not true."

"Good, then," said Nebuchadnezzar. "When you hear the horn, the pipe, the zither, the triangle, the dulcimer, and music and singing of all kinds, you will throw yourselves on your faces and worship the statue, or else I will throw you into a fiery furnace, and then God help you. What I mean is, even the gods can't help you then."

Again the three young men answered, "Don't be ridiculous. Of course we won't worship your statue. And you can do whatever you want to us; our God will be with us."

This made the king so angry that he ordered the furnace to be heated seven times hotter than usual. Then he ordered several strong soldiers to tie Shadrach, Meshach, and Abednego and throw them into the fiery furnace. The king had the furnace heated so hot that the soldiers who threw the three into it were reduced to ashes just by getting that close.

But when the king looked into the furnace, he shouted, "Didn't I order three people to be thrown into the fire? Why is it I see four? Get those three, uh, four—whatever, out and bring them here."

When Shadrach, Meshach, and Abednego were brought before the king, not only were they not burned, he couldn't even smell smoke on their clothes. Needless to say, Nebuchadnezzar was impressed. He ordered that no one speak a word against the God who had saved the three young men. In addition, the king made sure that Shadrach, Meshach, and Abednego were well provided for.

This story of three friends who stood up for their beliefs even at the risk of their lives includes a powerful portrayal of a God who is willing to walk through the fire with us. Many who have suffered for their faith have found great comfort in the story of Shadrach, Meshach, and Abednego.

There is something in this story for all ages. It is especially powerful for those who have had struggles, difficulties, and disappointments in their faith journeys, and for those who may be called upon to make tough decisions because of their faith.

II

Friends from the Greek Scriptures

The stories recorded in the New Testament have to do with the life of Jesus and the lives and thoughts of his friends. The people in the early Christian communities thought it was important to save these stories. For years they were passed on by word of mouth. The stories of Jesus and his friends were told in the whispers of those hiding for fear of their lives. They were told when Christians gathered in homes on the first day of the week to tell stories, sing songs, and share a meal in remembrance of the events of Jesus' life. Finally, they were told in loud voices by those we call martyrs, who gave up their lives because they had become friends of God through these stories.

After a number of years the stories were written down and collected in the books that Christians call the Gospels and the Acts of the Apostles, and in Paul's letters. Since that time they have been told again and again across the centuries and around the world. Persons of different languages, cultures, and nations have told these stories and deepened their friendship with God and one another by that telling and hearing.

Even today, as we hear and tell these stories, they can bring us to a deeper friendship with Jesus and those who were his first friends. As we hear the stories told to us by friends of other places and times, we strengthen our ties with those friends. We belong to a family of friends—friends of Jesus, friends of one another, friends of God.

8

The Birth of Jesus

Matthew 1:18-25
The Engaged Couple

An unmarried mother-to-be, a husband-to-be who is considering breaking off the marriage agreement, a hard-to-believe story about an angel, and troubled sleep—this is hardly the sentimental picture of Christmas we see in the store windows. Can God still surprise us by coming in such troubling ways?

It had been the most wonderful and terrible year of Joseph's life. It had been wonderful because he had become engaged to be married. His father had gone to her father to arrange it. When the fathers had agreed upon the bride-price to be paid to the woman's family, her father said to Joseph the words Saul had spoken to David: "You shall be my son-in-law." She was the choice Joseph would have made if he had done the choosing, though he had seen her only occasionally, carrying her jars to the public well for water or tending her family's sheep. She had a good strong name, Mary (Miriam, in their language). It was the name of the sister of Moses and Aaron. She could trace her family's ancestry back to King David, but then so could Joseph.

Two good families would come together in this marriage. It had been a wonderful year.

It had also been a terrible year. Shortly after the engagement was set, Mary had asked to see Joseph alone. It was highly unusual for an engaged couple to have time alone before they were married. That was when she told him the news. She was going to have a baby. Now, Joseph did not know much about such things, but the rabbis said that it took three to have a baby—a wife, a husband, and God. Mary told him that this time it had taken only two, and that he had been left out. It had been a terrible year.

Joseph was an honorable man and wanted to do the honorable thing in this situation. He had heard of such occurrences before and knew that it brought shame on the bride and her family, as well as on the groom and his family. So Joseph, accompanied by his own father, would offer to break the marriage contract privately. No one else would have to know.

Before he could put his plan into action, however, Joseph had a dream. It was the first night he had slept well. As he struggled with his decision concerning Mary and the marriage, he had tossed back and forth on his bed pallet there on the floor of his home. Nearby, the rest of his family slept soundly, innocent of Joseph's dilemma. Then, with his decision to end the engagement with Mary made, he slept and dreamed. In his dream a messenger of God appeared and told him, "Do not be afraid to take Mary as your wife, for this child is special. Do you remember in your classes at the synagogue hearing the passage in which the prophet Isaiah says to Ahaz the king, 'A child will be born to a young woman, and that child's name shall be called Immanuel, which means God with us'? This is the child of whom Isaiah spoke. When he is born you will name him Jesus [Yeshua, in Joseph's language], for he will save his people and all people from their sins." Even as he was waking, Joseph remembered thinking that the child of whom the prophet spoke was supposed to be a king, one who would free the people from their oppression. A king! From the family he and Mary would make? He was awakened by his own chuckling.

When he awoke fully, Joseph knew that he would marry Mary. Even if it was not the honorable thing to do, it was the right thing. Perhaps those two are not always the same. It was not simply a matter of trusting Mary; he hardly knew her. It was not even a matter of trusting the messenger; after all, it could have just been a dream. No, it was a matter of trusting this most surprising God. This was the God who promised Abraham and Sarah a child, then waited until they were old enough to be great-grandparents to give them one. Then this God asked Abraham to perform the most horrible of acts, to kill his son, his only son, promised by that same God. At the last moment, as the old man held the knife above the body of his son, God provided a ram to be sacrificed instead. Would Joseph too be asked to sacrifice this child? He shuddered at the thought.

So Joseph and Mary waited to see what this most surprising God would do.

Luke 1:39-56
Mary and Elizabeth

Here two women, friends and kinfolk, meet and understand each other in ways that no one else can. Mary's song is not an easy one. It tells of God overturning the world, lifting up the poor and oppressed and bringing down the powerful. It is a dangerous song that this young Jewish mother-to-be sings. Perhaps only one like her, or Hannah, could sing it. Perhaps only one like Elizabeth could understand it.

Only another woman would know—especially a member of the family. When Mary heard from the angel that Elizabeth too was going to have a child, she knew that she would have to see and speak with this older family member. No one would have expected this for either woman. There was Mary, without a husband—at least, not yet married, though promised to Joseph. And there was Elizabeth, who had been married for years to Zechariah; by now they were both far beyond the age for bearing children. The remarkable thing was that one as young and inexperienced as Mary and one who had spent as many childless years as Elizabeth would be adding members to the family. These were strange times indeed.

Mary wasn't sure if she was making this visit to help Elizabeth or to seek out the assistance of the more mature woman. But as she walked the dangerous and dusty roads traveling south from her home in Galilee toward the hill country of Judea, Mary had time to think. All along the way a particular story kept nudging its way into her memory. It was the memory of hearing about her ancestor Hannah, who like Elizabeth had spent many childless years before God had granted her a son, Samuel. Samuel had been the prophet who, though reluctant, had poured the oil of leadership on the head of King Saul and later King David. Would Elizabeth's child be a prophet? Would this child prepare for a new king, even the Messiah? It was too much to hope for, since during those days kings were not discovered by prophets at God's direction; they were appointed by the Romans.

All along the road, Hannah's song kept repeating in Mary's memory. She had heard her mother sing it as she had told the story. Its tune carried her along. God lifts up the poor and the needy from the dust and the ash heaps of the world and places them in seats of honor, even with royalty, it said. As it repeated in her imagination the song began to change, to become her song. She would sing it to Elizabeth when she told her of the unexpected blessing she too was expectant with.

Mary entered the house where Elizabeth and Zechariah lived, and the two women embraced in greeting. Suddenly, the older woman pulled away as if she had experienced a pain. But there was no sign of discomfort on her face. She smiled at Mary as she said, "Blessed are you among women and blessed is the fruit of your womb," and told of the way her own child had moved inside her at the sound of Mary's voice.

Now it was time. Mary sang her song, that was Hannah's song, and Elizabeth's song, and the song of all their people who longed to see the proud scattered and the mighty taken from their thrones. God had remembered these two, a girl too young and a woman too old, and through them had remembered all the people who lived beyond the edge of the expected. So Mary stayed with Elizabeth for three months. They each took care of the other, as only women who know are able.

Here are two very different versions of the events surrounding Jesus' birth. The first is told by a narrator looking over Joseph's shoulder; the second presents the situation from Mary's point of view.

I personally like to preserve the distinctive qualities of each of the two versions found in Matthew and Luke, rather than mix them together as we often choose to do.

The first of these stories I told as a part of a longer story-sermon on Matthew's nativity narrative at two small country churches. The pastor of those churches had asked me to preach for her during her maternity leave. She sat there listening, due to deliver her own child at any moment. Her little girl was born on Christmas morning, and I was privileged to spend the next Sunday at the same churches celebrating both the birth of Christ and their pastor's and her husband's new daughter. Look for these special occasions to tell certain stories, and welcome them whenever they arise.

The story from Luke includes a stirring song that echoes the song sung by Hannah when she was finally able to give birth to a child after years of waiting (I Samuel 1:1–2:11). You may wish to tell both stories side by side so your listeners can hear both the similarities and differences between them.

Another way to let each story speak for itself would be to ask a man to tell Joseph's version and a woman to tell Mary's.

9

Lost and Found

Luke 2:41-52
Mary, Joseph, and Jesus

*Do you remember as a child what it felt like to lose sight of
your parents in the grocery store or the churchyard? Or have
you ever lost a child or a pet? Now can you imagine what
Mary and Joseph were feeling when they discovered Jesus was
missing?*

Mary was frantic. She and Joseph had searched the streets of
Jerusalem for almost three days. They had come with family
and neighbors to celebrate the Passover in the Holy City. It
seemed as if everyone else in the world had the same idea. The
streets were so crowded with people it was difficult to move
through them.

Now that the festival had ended, many of the crowds had
gone, but Jerusalem was a large city and no place for a young
boy. After all, Jesus was only twelve years old. In her worst
moments Mary had visions of him begging for food in rags
from some doorway or, even more frightening, lying dead
somewhere in the maze of streets.

Beneath her fear, Mary was angry. She was angry at Jesus for
not leaving the city with the family. She was angry with herself

and Joseph for waiting all day, until the whole group they were traveling with had camped for the night, to look for their son. Of course, they had thought he was safe. Of course, they had expected him to be with some other family, playing with cousins his age. Of course, no one blamed them. It was understandable.

Understandable, yes! But the fact remained that twelve-year-old Jesus was lost . . . in a large and dangerous city . . . alone. It was the third day of the search, and there had been no sign of their son. Then, as Joseph and Mary walked through one of the public areas of the temple, they heard a voice that caused them both to gasp with expectation—the voice of their son. There he was, sitting among the teachers with their long robes and long beards who nodded as the boy answered their questions.

Mary ran to them, and her sharp voice cut off the conversation in mid-sentence. "What in the world were you thinking, young man? Your father and I have been half out of our minds with grief, looking for you."

Jesus looked up at her as if she were a total stranger. Then he said the strangest thing. "Why were you both so worried? Didn't you know I would be right here at home?"

Though his answer made no sense, relief had replaced the anger in Mary's heart. She took her son from among the teachers, and she and Joseph and Jesus returned to Nazareth, where Jesus tried never to worry his parents like that again.

Though Mary did not understand what had taken place in the temple that day, she kept the memories in her heart. From time to time in her silent moments, she would take them out and look at them in her imagination as if they were precious treasures.

Jesus grew strong in body and wise in learning, loved by both God and his neighbors.

What parent has not experienced the panic and helplessness that Mary and Joseph know in this story? This is truly a story for children and adults alike, though parents of young children may find it most immediately applicable to their situation.

You may wish to have this story told by a family. For an interesting twist, have children portray the adults and an adult portray Jesus.

Or, this story may be introduced by having parents and children tell stories of getting separated from one another and of the feeling each of them experienced.

10

Encounters with Jesus

Luke 7:36-50
Jesus, a Man, and a Woman

Have you ever hurt or betrayed a friend and wondered if you could ever be forgiven? The woman in this story seems to be worried about just that. In an unfriendly house, she finds a friend.

Once Jesus was invited to the house of a very religious man for dinner. When Jesus entered he was not greeted properly and was treated as such a stranger that anyone else would have been insulted and left. But Jesus stayed.

Just as those gathered at the very religious man's home were visiting, a woman walked in from the street. Now, according to the talk around town she was not the kind of person who would ever in a million years be invited to such a dinner. But in she walked and went directly to Jesus. She began to talk with him, and as she talked she began to cry. As the woman cried, her tears fell on the feet of the only one in the room who would talk to her. As her tears wet Jesus' feet she began to kiss them, then dry them with her hair. When she had finished, she took an expensive jar of perfumed oil and poured it over his feet.

The very religious man thought to himself, "Well, I wonder

just how this 'Teacher' knows this woman? And if he does, why in the world would he allow her to even talk with him, much less to be as intimate as she has been?"

The very religious man's face must have betrayed his thoughts, because Jesus spoke up and said, "Simon, I want to tell you a story."

"Yes, Teacher." Simon condemned Jesus' behavior with the very title.

Jesus began, "Two people owed money to another, a lender of money. One of the two owed the lender fifty dollars, while the other owed ten times as much. Neither one could pay, so the lender forgave both debts. Which one do you suppose will appreciate the lender more?"

"This is too easy," thought Simon; "there must be a trick." But there was only one answer: "The one to whom he forgave the largest debt, I suppose."

"Exactly right!" Jesus told Simon. "I came into your home at your invitation and was treated like a stranger. You offered no servant to wash my feet, as I might have expected. But you see my friend here. She has washed my feet with her tears and dried them with her hair and treated me like a friend rather than a stranger. You provided not one drop of oil for my head, as a guest might expect, but my friend here has literally covered my feet with perfume, as a friend might expect. When I came to your door at your request, there was no kiss of greeting waiting for me, as a guest might expect, but my friend here has not stopped kissing my feet, something even a friend would not expect. You may think she is a bad person for her life in the past, but I tell you her great love proves that her sins have been forgiven."

Then he looked Simon directly in the eye. "But those who think they need no forgiveness show very little love."

Then Jesus looked at his friend and said, "Your love and friendship have proved your sins are forgiven."

The other very religious people at Simon's house began to murmur, "Just who does he think he is, forgiving sins like that?"

But Jesus must not have been listening to them. He

continued speaking to his friend: "Your love and friendship are signs of your faith that has saved you. Shalom—peace."

Luke 8:26-39

Jesus and the Demons

Jesus befriended many people who felt friendless. The man in the following story seems bent on destroying himself, propelled by forces he cannot control. Jesus is friend to the man in the story. Is it possible that Jesus even befriended the Many Beyond Number, whose request he granted?

There was a man who lived with his family in one of the cities of the Decapolis. One day he began to be filled with feelings he did not understand. One moment he would begin laughing and be unable to stop. Then he would begin to cry and not be able to control his crying. His moods would swing from joy to depression without warning. It was as if he were not one person but was filled with different people. When he began to be filled with these personalities, the pressure would build inside him until it became almost unbearable.

He was forced to leave his family and seek out a place to live far from other people. He finally moved in among the tombs carved from the side of a hill along the shore of the Sea of Galilee. "After all, I might as well be dead," he thought. Often when people would pass that way, he would begin to feel the pressure of the many persons who lived inside him filling him, until he would run forth from the tomb shouting at the passers-by. He would pick up the sharp chips of flint rock that lay everywhere along the hillside and cut his body in an attempt to relieve the pressure. For a time it would be relieved. Others had attempted to chain the man to the walls of the tomb, but when the persons who lived inside him filled him, he had had such strength that he broke the chains.

57

One day Jesus and some of his friends came by that way in a boat on the Sea of Galilee. As Jesus looked up toward the tombs, he saw the man. When the man saw Jesus looking toward him, he ran from his tomb shouting and cutting himself with the sharp flint chips. He felt the pressure of the many persons who lived inside him, and this time the pressure would not be relieved. The man shouted in a voice not his own, "What have you to do with me, O Chosen One of God!"

Hearing the pain in the voice that called out, Jesus spoke to the man, asking, "What is your name?"

Again the voice that was not his own replied, "We are many, beyond number. We are Legion."

There was a herd of pigs feeding along the water's edge nearby. When the Many Beyond Number saw the pigs, they begged Jesus not to send them into nothingness but to send them into the herd. Again Jesus heard the pain in the voice that spoke, and he called for the Many Beyond Number to come out of the man and enter the herd of pigs. When this happened, the pigs ran headlong into the sea and drowned.

Those who had been watching over the herd hurried to tell their neighbors what had happened. When the neighbors heard the reports from the herders, they returned to Jesus and told him to leave that place because they were afraid. Jesus and all those gathered saw that the man who had once shouted at them and cut himself had returned to the person he was before the Many had entered him. As Jesus started to leave, the man asked to go with the friends who followed Jesus. But Jesus told him, "No, go back to your family and your city and tell them all that has been done for you."

Matthew 15:21-28

Jesus and a Foreign Woman

This story troubles many religious people because in it a foreign woman reminds Jesus of what he has spoken and acted out in his better moments. Can the truly human Jesus be corrected by an outsider, a woman not of his faith?

One day as Jesus was traveling through an area near the cities of Tyre and Sidon, a woman from that place, a Canaanite, came following after him. She kept shouting, "Help me! Have mercy on me! Please, my daughter is terribly ill. She is not herself. Some say her body has been taken over by a demon. Please, won't you help me?"

Jesus seemed not to notice that she was there. He did not look at her or say a word. The friends who were with him finally begged him, "Get her out of here. She is making too much noise. People are looking at us. They will think she is with our group."

When Jesus looked at the woman, he saw in her face what he had heard in her speech—she was not of his religion. But she was terribly upset. He said to her, "You have the wrong person. I came to seek the lost sheep of Israel, not Canaan."

Hearing these words, the woman threw herself on the ground at Jesus' feet, pleading with him, "Please help me, kind sir."

A bit irritated with her now, Jesus said, "You do not take the food away from the children and throw it to the dogs." To call someone a dog was an insult. Jesus knew that. The words sounded harsh, lacking compassion.

The woman looked directly at Jesus and answered, "That is very true, even in the house of a Canaanite woman, but we do let the dogs eat what falls from the table after the meal."

Suddenly the wall that Jesus' insult had placed between him and the woman came crashing down because of her words—an answer steeped in wisdom from one who was not of his faith. He knew it now. The bread was for her as well.

"What faith you have!" Jesus' voice was no longer irritated. "Go in peace; your request has been granted." After that, the woman's daughter was herself again.

Luke 19:1-10
Jesus and Zacchaeus

It is easier to imagine Jesus befriending a poor person or a sick person than a rich and powerful person who has cheated his neighbors to gain his station in life. In this story Jesus reaches out to a tax collector, hated by his neighbors because he has cheated them to enrich himself and the Roman government. How do you think you would feel if you were one of his neighbors, watching this scene?

Jericho was a city of beautiful houses and balsam groves, the winter capitol built by Herod. It was a wealthy city that lay where the canyon called Wadi Quelt opened into the fertile Jordan Valley. Among the wealthiest of its people were the tax collectors. They bought their jobs from the Romans, and as long as they collected the amount of money and goods the Romans wanted, they could keep anything over and above that for themselves.

Among the wealthiest of the tax collectors was the chief collector who supervised all the others. His name was Zacchaeus.

One day Jesus came passing through Jericho on his way toward Jerusalem. Zacchaeus wanted to see this Teacher, but the crowds were so large and so close that he could not see. Zacchaeus climbed a tree in order to see the Teacher.

When Jesus saw the man in the tree, he approached and called, "Zacchaeus, come right down here. Today I will eat at your house."

Zacchaeus climbed down, and together he and the Teacher went to his house. As they passed through the crowd, both could hear the grumbling.

"He's going to eat at that tax collector's house."

"Eat with a filthy, lying cheat of a tax collector, will you?"

"He's too good to eat with honest folk like us. No, he has to go to the big shot's house!"

Once at Zacchaeus's house, the tax collector was moved by

Jesus' concern for him and said, "Right here and now I promise half of all I own to the poor."

"We'll believe that when we see it"—someone from the crowd spoke the words they all felt.

"And if I have cheated any people—" Zacchaeus continued.

"If! Did you hear that? 'If I have cheated,' he says," another voice from the crowd responded.

"—I will repay them four times what I took from them." Zacchaeus made a rash promise that no one expected him to keep.

Then Jesus spoke. "Today those in this household have come alive. This tax collector is as much a child of God as any of you are. You see, the one God sent came to look after those people everyone else considers to be lost causes."

From there Jesus made his way along the road toward Jerusalem, and all that waited for him there.

These four stories are about Jesus' relationships with other people, especially those who were not considered acceptable by the good religious people of the time.

It is likely that these stories will have a very different impact if told to the good religious people who gather in our churches than if told to those considered outcasts in our society, such as those in prisons, rescue missions, or AIDS wards.

These are stories of reaching. In them Jesus reaches out beyond the boundaries of the acceptable to invite into friendship those who stand on the other side.

Warning: These stories might just drive the one telling them outside the boundaries of what is acceptable today, following the example of the storyteller, Jesus.

11

Jesus, the Storyteller

Matthew 20:1-16

The Vineyard Owner and the Workers

This is only one of the many stories Jesus told about what life is like under God's reign. If you were one of the first hired, how do you think you would feel? What if you were one of the last ones hired; how would you feel then? Is this really the way God works with us?

The reign of God is like someone who owned a vineyard when the grapes were coming ripe. If they were not picked just at the right time, there would be no use picking them at all. So the vineyard owner went into the marketplace, where all the people looking for work would gather, and began to hire workers. The owner asked who would work picking grapes all day for a silver coin. Well, a silver coin was all anyone could expect to earn in those days for a full day's work. It would provide food for a day. Several agreed to that wage and were sent to work in the vineyard.

Several hours later, at midmorning, the owner returned to the marketplace and saw some other people standing around. He asked them, "Will you come and work for me picking the grapes in my vineyard? I will pay you what is fair." So those too went to work.

The vineyard owner passed through the marketplace again at the middle of the day and in the middle of the afternoon and hired other workers. Then late in the afternoon, just before quitting time, the owner made one more pass through the marketplace. There were still people standing around waiting to be hired. The owner asked them, "What? Hasn't anyone hired you?"

"No one would have us," they answered.

As he looked at them, the owner knew why they had not been hired. These were always the first hired and the first let go from work.

"Well, I'll hire you to pick grapes for me." And the owner took them to the vineyard for the last hour of work.

When it came time for everyone to be paid, the owner told the steward who would be paying them that they should line up in a certain order to receive their pay. The last hired would be at the front of the line, and the first hired would wait until last to be paid.

Each worker was paid one silver coin, a day's wages. When those who had worked only one hour began to walk down the line, those who had been hired first saw that the last had been paid a full day's wages, and they began to dream aloud. "If the owners paid them one silver piece for working one hour, what will we receive for working all day?"

But their dreams began to fade as they watched all the workers passing by them one by one taking home only one silver coin. When those who had worked all day received their silver coin, they were angry. They went to the owner to complain.

"We worked all day in the hot sun picking your grapes," they grumbled, "then we got paid exactly what those who worked only one hour in the cool of the day were paid. Is that fair?"

The owner listened until the complaints were finished. "What did you agree to work for this morning? Was it one silver coin or not?"

They had to admit they had agreed to that wage.

"Then take your pay and move along," the owner told them. "I haven't cheated you out of anything, because you received exactly what we agreed upon. But I have chosen to pay everyone else, even those hired for one hour, the same wage—enough to buy food for their families for one day. Are you suggesting that I have no right to be generous with what is mine?"

Then Jesus ended his story: "Those who are last in these times will be first in the reign of God, and those who are first in these times will be last in the reign of God."

This is just one of the stories remembered by the early Christian communities as having been told by Jesus. On the surface it may appear simple and straightforward, but from beneath the surface of the story we hear rumblings that warn us that the very foundations of our comfortable world are about to be shaken. A teller needs to do some homework to tell these stories well. When you encounter a parable of Jesus', it will help to find a good Bible dictionary and look up those persons, places, or things mentioned in the story with which you are unfamiliar. In fact, it is a good idea to do this sort of study before telling any biblical story. There are people, places, and things in them that those who heard the story when it was first told would have understood, but that we no longer know about. How much a denarius was worth, what was a Samaritan or Pharisee, and how tax collectors got their jobs and made a living are just a few such concerns.

Here are some other stories of this type:

Luke 15:1-10	*The lost sheep and lost coin*
Luke 15:11-32	*The loving father*
Luke 18:9-14	*The Pharisee and the tax collector*
Matthew 13:44-46	*The hidden treasure, the pearl of great price, the net*
Matthew 18:23-35	*The merciless servant*

Another word of warning: The stories Jesus told about how different things will be under God's reign may have been one of the reasons he angered people so greatly that they crucified him. We good workers, good people, good church folk may have to adjust the most when things begin to change.

12

Friends of Jesus

Matthew 26:17-25, 47-56; 27:1-10
Jesus and Judas

*Judas betrayed Jesus, but the story tells us that the other
disciples betrayed him in their own way as well. Only the
women who followed Jesus remained by his side throughout
his ordeal. If Jesus forgave Peter and the others, is it possible
that he forgave Judas too?*

It was the perfect friendship—almost. Jesus trusted Judas
with the group's treasury because apparently Judas had a way
with money. As the women who followed the Rabbi from
Nazareth contributed more and more of their personal funds
to buy bread, wine, and other necessities for the group,
someone was needed to take care of the finances. Jesus chose
Judas for this job.

Not only was Judas trusted with the money, he seems to have
had special privileges within the group. At the last meal Jesus
would eat with his disciples before his death, he gave Judas the
place of honor at the table. As they all reclined around the
table, the conversation makes it clear that Judas lay next to
Jesus. He tore bread from the same loaf and dipped it into the
same bowl as the Rabbi. Propped on his left elbow, Jesus could

lean back and lay his head on Judas's chest, speaking to this one disciple without the others hearing.

"One of you will betray me," Jesus spoke to the entire group. Each one gathered there thought it could be him. But Judas felt the words fall heavily on his chest, and he continued to breathe only with great difficulty.

"One who dipped his hand in the bowl with me"—the words were directed to Judas this time. Judas's face flushed hot, and he wished in that instant that he had never been born.

"Surely you don't mean me, Rabbi?" The words fell heavy as silver from Judas's tongue. He almost didn't hear the response.

"The words are yours." Jesus turned back to the group, who were still discussing whether it might be one of them. He broke bread, gave thanks, and gave it to them all. "Take this and eat it. It is my body broken for you."

"He knows," Judas thought without speaking. "He knows that I have taken money to turn him in, and yet he still eats with me." To eat with another was a sign that all was forgiven. "Can an action be forgiven even before the deed is done?" Judas wondered. After taking the bread as it passed and drinking from the cup, they all arose singing and left that place. Judas slipped away from the group and blended into the night.

Later, in the garden, Jesus would tell all the other disciples that they would all betray him. But Judas was not there to hear these words. He must have thought he was the only one.

When Judas returned, he saw Jesus for the last time, said, "Peace, Rabbi" for the last time, pressed cheek to cheek and beard to beard, kissing him, for the last time, and heard Jesus call him "friend" for the last time, even while telling him to do quickly what he had to do. Surrounded by people carrying clubs and swords, prepared to put him to death, Jesus spoke words of peace, as Judas somehow knew he would. After the crowd took Jesus away, all the disciples deserted and betrayed him.

Soon the word came to Judas that Jesus had been condemned. That was not what he had intended, not what he had planned. Things had gotten out of hand, out of Judas's control. He tried to give the money back, the money he had been given to take the authorities to Jesus. But they would not have it back. He threw the coins on the floor and ran from that place. He could not turn back and undo what he had done. "How could it ever be forgiven?" his mind cried out with remorse. Forgetting that last forgiving meal that Jesus shared with all the disciples who would betray him—Judas, Peter, and the others—Judas went to a lonely place and hanged himself.

The money he threw away was used to buy from a potter a field in which foreigners would be buried. They called the field Akeldama, the field of blood.

John 20:24-29

Jesus and Thomas

Thomas was bluntly honest with Jesus and his other friends. He is an example of telling the truth in love. Can you be as honest about your faith and doubts as Thomas was?

Thomas was just too honest for his own good. Whatever came to his mind just jumped right out of his mouth. When Jesus was determined to return to the place where his very life had been threatened to see his friends Mary and Martha and their brother Lazarus, who had fallen ill, Thomas spoke up: "Let us go too so we might die with you." It is not clear whether the other disciples were pleased when Thomas included them in his rash acts of loyalty. But there you have it—that was Thomas.

Later, as Jesus attempted to prepare his disciples for the time when he would not be with them, he told them that he was going to prepare a place for them. Where he went they would go, and he went on to say that they all knew where that was. Well, Thomas said out loud what everybody else was thinking. "How in the world are we supposed to know where you are going? How are we supposed to know the way?" Just a little too forthright for his own good, this Thomas was.

Did you ever notice in the story, as John tells it, that when Jesus appears to the disciples after the resurrection, they are all in hiding for fear of their lives, except for Thomas? Was he the only one brave enough to go out? We don't know, but he wasn't there.

So it's not too difficult to understand his response when the others said they had seen Jesus. "Right," he told them, "and I'm the Queen of Sheba. I'll believe that when I see him—when I put my fingers in the holes the nails left in his hands and my hand in the gash in his side." It wasn't that he didn't trust Jesus. He just wasn't sure he wanted to take the word of a bunch of cowards on such an important matter.

Eight days later Jesus paid them another visit. The only difference was that this time Thomas was there. Jesus greeted them: "Shalom, peace." He went right over to Thomas and offered him his hands and his side. Jesus didn't tell Thomas he was wrong or bad. He just told him, "I want you to know what these others know."

To that Thomas said, "Now *this* is my Lord and my God."

Then Jesus told him, "If you think this is a blessing to you who have seen me, just think of all those who will come after you who will be blessed even though they never saw me."

Maybe the only one in the whole crowd who was more honest than Thomas was Jesus himself.

Luke 24:13-35

Jesus and His Friends at Emmaus

Jesus' friends knew him when he ate with them. In the ancient world eating with someone was a sign of forgiveness and friendship. How can we share the friendship of Jesus in the hurried and frantic rush of modern mealtimes?

Two of those who had followed Jesus during his lifetime were walking down the road toward a village called Emmaus.

69

As they walked the seven miles from Jerusalem, they talked of the terrifying and baffling events of the past several days. While they walked and talked, someone joined them on the road, someone they did not recognize.

"I couldn't help but overhear your conversation and notice how sadly you walk along. What has happened that makes you so sad and fearful?" their companion asked the two.

"Are you new in town, or what? Haven't you heard what's happened the past few days? You must be the only one who hasn't heard," Cleopas replied.

"What things?" the stranger asked.

"About our Teacher, Jesus of Nazareth." The two rushed to tell their traveling companion what had happened. "He was a prophet if ever there was one, one who spoke the truth and did what was right before God and the people. But those in power had him put to death. He was crucified."

Their voices slowed. "Now it has been three days." The next words were almost a sign: "We had hoped he was the Chosen One of God, the one who would set the people free."

The other picked up the story. "Some of the women who followed him told us the most astounding thing. They had gone to his tomb to complete the burial process when they saw a vision of angels or something telling them he was not dead but alive. Then when they looked into the tomb, they saw the graveclothes but not his body."

Then the stranger surprised the two with what he said. "How slow some are to hear what the prophets have said! The Chosen One of God had to suffer all that you have said before freedom could come to the people."

Was this some wandering teacher, the two wondered? But they did not say a word. They simply listened as their companion told stories about the Chosen One of God from the Scriptures. And as they listened, they slowly began to understand.

When they arrived at Emmaus, it looked as if the stranger was going farther down the road. But it was already evening, so the two invited their walking companion to join them for the night. As all three sat down to eat, the stranger broke the bread

70

and said the blessing, "Baruch ata, Adonai Eloheinu . . ." As the words rolled out of his mouth, the two suddenly recognized him. It was Jesus. When they looked again, however, he was gone.

The two looked at each other and said, "We should have known. The delight that burned in our hearts as he told us those stories . . . We should have known then, but it was not until he broke bread with us that we really saw him for who he was."

So they went to the other followers of Jesus and told them, "What the women told us is true. He walked with us along the road, but we did not know him until he broke bread with us."

Jesus attracted a diverse group of friends—tax collectors, prostitutes, and political revolutionaries, to name just a few. These stories are about several very different friends of Jesus, each with a very distinct personality.

These stories are especially important to tell for those who, for some reason or other, do not feel worthy of God's love and Jesus' friendship. Like the bread and cup at Holy Communion, this love and friendship are for those who don't feel worthy. In fact, these are good stories to tell in preparation for receiving communion.

Such stories of Jesus' friendship with outcasts are always appropriate to tell on visits to nursing homes, hospitals, or prisons.

13

Early Followers

Acts 10
Peter and Cornelius

Whom does your church tell you not to associate with? Who is considered to be outside the faith because of beliefs or life-style? Imagine going to visit such people, talking with them and eating with them and accepting them as your friends. How would you feel? How would your church friends feel about you when they found out? Now you have some idea of the way Peter feels in this story.

Peter could not believe that he had even set foot inside the house. Here he was in a Gentile city named for Caesar, Caesarea. As if that were not bad enough, he was standing in the doorway of the house of a Gentile, speaking with its owner—a clear violation of religious law. And as if *that* were not bad enough, the owner of the house was not just a Gentile, he was an officer in the Roman army, the commander of a group of approximately one hundred of the soldiers who occupied Peter's homeland.

He was violating custom, law, even loyalty to his country by standing in that entryway. The first words out of his mouth, after he had made his host get up off the floor and stop bowing before him as if Peter were some god or dignitary, were "You know it is against my religion to be here with you." The words seemed rude and intolerant in Peter's ears even as he spoke them.

Then why was he there? Well, he had come at the request of Cornelius, the Roman officer, who had sent people down the coast to Joppa to invite Peter to his house. But why did he accept the invitation? Well, that's another story.

Peter had been on the roof of the house of a man named Simon, a tanner in whose house he had been a guest in Joppa. As the time came near for the midday meal and his stomach began to growl, Peter experienced what might be described as a waking dream.

In the dream he saw a sheet full of creatures being lowered down from the sky to the roof on which he was praying. The only problem was that all these creatures were those that his religion forbade him to eat. A voice surrounded him, saying, "Take and eat."

"Lord," Peter responded, "no unclean thing has ever so much as touched my lips." For a time Peter thought his hunger was driving him to see things.

But twice more the sheet full of creatures was lowered. And twice more Peter refused these "unclean" foods. Then the voice added something that shocked this good, religious man. It said, "Do not call unclean what God has called clean."

Just then, another voice called Peter back to himself, telling him to come downstairs, he had visitors. They were the messengers Cornelius had sent. Had it not been for the waking dream, it is likely that he would never have accepted such an invitation.

All along the way, as Peter thought to himself, "I have never visited the house of a Gentile before," the voice came back to him: "Do not call unclean what God has called clean."

So standing in the company of Gentiles, Peter spoke to them of his own change of heart when he said, "I now understand that God does not play favorites. Instead, anyone of any background who stands in awe of God and does what is right is accepted." He then told those gathered stories about Jesus, and when he was finished he ate food he had once considered unclean, with those he had once thought of as unclean. And because God had shown favor to those gathered in Cornelius's house that day, Peter baptized them as well.

When he returned home to Jerusalem, there were many who thought Peter had done wrong. He had to answer many questions about what he was doing and what he had done at the house of Cornelius. Soon after, the communities that claimed loyalty to Jesus would have to decide if they were going to call unclean those whom God had called clean.

Peter's (and later Paul's) understanding won the day, and a bridge was built between two groups, each of whom had thought the other unclean. Perhaps that is the reason that to this day Peter's successors as Bishop of Rome are called *Pontifex,* "builder of bridges."

Acts 9:26-30; 15:36-41

Barnabas, Paul, and John Mark

> *Barnabas gives Saul a second chance when others are not so sure they should. Then he gives John Mark a second chance when Saul (now Paul) is not willing to. How do you think the members of the church felt when Barnabas suggested that they accept Saul even though he had been persecuting them? How do you think Paul felt when Barnabas gave John Mark another chance? Who has given you a second chance? When have you given someone else a second chance? When have you refused to give a second chance to someone?*

His name was Barnabas, "son of encouragement." Some might call him "the Saint of Second Chances." Take, for example, Saul of Tarsus, who had persecuted the followers of Jesus and even stood by while one of them, Stephen, was stoned to death. When Saul came to the community of believers in Jerusalem, saying that he had experienced a change of heart and that he wanted to join with them, many opposed him. Some were suspicious of him, for they feared that it was a trick, while others just feared the man because of what he had done in the past. But Barnabas spoke up, suggesting that they give him a second chance, and took him by the hand and led him to the apostles. On the suggestion of Barnabas, they allowed Saul to stay with the community.

Perhaps it was because Barnabas was himself an outsider, having been born in Cyprus. Or it may have been that he was one of the Greek-speaking members of the Jewish community and understood what it was like to be misunderstood. We do not know. But he must have been an impressive figure, because after he and Saul, now called Paul, began to travel together, Barnabas got top billing among those who told stories of the two. In fact, when they were both in a town called Lystra, where the people were more familiar with the Greek gods than the God of the Hebrew and Christian communities, the people compared Barnabas and Paul to gods. Paul was like Hermes, the speaker and messenger of the gods, but Barnabas, they seemed sure, was Zeus, king of the gods. It took some explaining to convince those who heard that the two were mere human beings.

At Jerusalem, when a discussion arose about whether Gentiles must become Jews to become Christians, Barnabas and Paul were on the same side of the argument. They both believed, along with Peter, that Gentiles were to be welcomed just as they were. Barnabas and Paul even carried a letter to the church at Antioch saying as much.

Finally, Barnabas and Paul came to a parting of the ways. Barnabas suggested that they return to all the cities they had visited and see how the churches were doing there. Paul was agreeable to that, except that Barnabas wanted to take John Mark along. Earlier John Mark had gone with them to Cyprus and for some unknown reason left them before the time there was finished. Paul was against taking him along again.

Barnabas pleaded for John Mark the same way he had spoken before the community at Jerusalem on Saul's behalf. "Give him a second chance," Barnabas argued. But Paul, apparently forgetting that those same words had been spoken to plead his own case, would not hear of it.

So Paul and Silas departed, traveling toward Syria. Barnabas, along with John Mark, sailed for Cyprus. When in later years

Paul wrote about Barnabas, he did not mention what happened at Jerusalem or with John Mark. He said only that he and Barnabas both worked for a living—worked separately, that is.

Both of these stories about Peter and Cornelius and Paul and Barnabas were told in somewhat longer versions as sermons, but in their brief tellings they could provide a devotion for a missions or evangelism committee meeting, or be included in a class on personalities from the early Christian communities.

The first hesitant step by Peter into the home of the Roman soldier is a great leap toward inclusiveness for the early followers of Jesus. Though he was technically breaking religious law as he understood it, in a real sense Peter was following in the footsteps of Jesus. This story is appropriate for any situation in which there are clearly insiders and outsiders. Realize, though, that each of those groups will probably respond to the story differently.

Barnabas is "the Saint of Second Chances." He urged the followers of Jesus to give Saul, their persecutor, a second chance. Later, when Saul, now Paul, refused to give John Mark a second chance, who should take him on as a partner in ministry but Barnabas. This is a perfect story for families, in which there is always a need for second and third and even more chances.

III

Friends from Many Times

Our friends are not always flesh and blood human beings. Often, characters in stories we have heard become for us companions on our journeys. The traditions of our faith are filled with the stories of friends from legend and history. One is not necessarily more important than the other.

Sometimes the stories comment on and flesh out stories from Scripture, such as the legends surrounding the Christmas story. Others, like the stories of Francis or Patrick, provide for us models as we struggle to live our faith.

The characters in stories live and walk around inside us. They become part of a community that lives in our imaginations. The love we have for them is real, and the ways of friendship they teach us are valuable.

14

Tales of Christmas

Luke 2:1-7
Jesus and the Stork

What do we mean when we ask if a story is true? Most often we are asking if it "really happened." Yet there are stories that never happened in a historical sense but carry with them a ring of truth. Jesus' parables are examples of created stories that are nevertheless true. The Christmas legends that follow speaks the truth of the heart, not just the truth of the eye.

On the night Jesus was born, the stork, who was standing nearby, noticed that there was no place for Mary to lay the baby down to rest. The only place that was anything like a cradle or a bed was a large stone manger, a feeding trough for animals. So Mary laid the baby Jesus on a bed of rough straw in that manger. As the stork continued to watch, she noticed that the baby could not go to sleep on so rough a bed. So the stork began to pluck feathers from her own breast and place them one by one on the straw for the child to rest upon. Soon there was a soft bed of stork feathers covering the straw. On this bed of stork feathers Jesus slept restfully through the night. But now the stork's breast was plucked clean of feathers. Mary, the mother of Jesus, stroked the stork's breast, blessed the bird, and declared that from that day forward the stork would be the bird associated with the birth of children. And so to this day people speak of storks bringing children.

Isaiah 9:6-7

Enemies and the Mistletoe

Recall a time when someone shared Christ's peace with you. Perhaps no words were exchanged. No worship was being conducted. There was neither music nor lightning, nor did the earth move. Perhaps that peace was offered by a glance, a touch, or a smile. Each time this happens, the story of the mistletoe is told again.

Do you know what people do under the mistletoe at Christmas? Of course you do. They kiss. But do you know why they kiss? Well, long ago the Roman people saw mistletoe growing in trees, without any roots or connection to the earth, and they thought that this plant must be very special. In fact, they considered it such a special plant that warring armies that happened to meet under the mistletoe were expected to make peace. And whenever generals made peace, they often chose to do so under the mistletoe, to show that they meant to keep that peace. Is it any wonder, then, that during the season when we celebrate the birth of the one called "Prince of Peace" that friends kiss and share other signs of peace under the mistletoe?

Matthew 1:18-25

Jesus and the Robin

Imagine the ordinary surroundings into which Jesus was born. The ordinary tales that surround that very special event testify that it was not only humankind but all creation that celebrated the birth of the Christ. In this way even an ordinary bird becomes a reminder of God's love born into the world.

Legend has it that at the birth of Jesus there was a robin among the other animals and birds in the stable. Now, the robin then was not as we know the robin today. No, the robin near the manger that night was a plain gray bird—as all robins were in those days. As the night passed and the other animals and people drifted off to sleep, the robin remained awake. She watched the small fire that provided the only warmth for human and animal alike. In the wee hours of the morning, after all the others had long been asleep, the robin watched the flame of the fire grow smaller and smaller until all that was left was a pile of glowing coals. Fearing that the newborn baby might catch a chill, the robin flew into the fire, flapping her wings furiously. The stir of wind she created made the fire flame higher—but only for a little while. Soon there were only coals left as the fire died. Again and again, throughout the night, the courageous bird flew into the fire to keep it burning. The baby Jesus slept on straw wrapped in swaddling cloths and warmed by that small fire. The next morning everyone awoke to find something that surprised them. Not only had the fire continued to burn throughout the night, but something about the robin had changed. By flying into the fire to keep it burning and the newborn warm, she had singed her breast. It was no longer a dull gray; it had turned bright red. And so it is to this day.

Isaiah 11:1-6

A Child and a Flower

Stories from cultures not our own can fling open the doors of our imaginations to experiences and understandings we would never come to otherwise. The following story in its essentials is found in a number of settings. This is my favorite.

There is a flower that is associated with Christmas in the United States called the poinsettia, but in Mexico the flower goes by a different name—*la flor de la noche buena* ("the flower of the good night," that is, Christmas Eve night).

In Mexico people tell of an orphan boy who lived on a ranch three days journey from Mexico City. After both his parents had died, the boy was taken in by the owner of the ranch to live and work with the people there. The ranch became home to the boy, and its people were his family.

From his youngest days the boy kept a special memory and a secret hope in his heart. He recalled that when he had been a small boy, his parents had taken him to Mexico City on Christmas Eve night for the midnight worship service. This service was called the *Misa del gallo* (the "mass of the rooster"), and some people told a story that when the Christ Child was born, a rooster crowed to announce the birth to the world. At the end of that service all the people brought to the altar gifts for the Christ Child. The boy's secret hope was to return to that service one Christmas Eve and take a present of his own to the front of the church.

When the boy was nearly thirteen years old, he was called into the hacienda in which the old man lived. The boy entered the main house and looked across a long room to where the owner was seated at a large, dark wooden table. The old man called the boy to come stand near him and said he had a favor to ask. The ranch needed someone to represent it at the *Misa del gallo* at Christmas. Did the boy think he was old enough to be trusted to go? "Yes!" The word leapt from his throat as he thought it. The man reached into a small leather pouch, took out a five-peso piece, and handed the coin to the boy. It was money to buy a present for the Christ Child. The boy danced out of the hacienda to tell all his friends on the ranch.

When the day came for the boy to leave, his friends had baked bread for him to eat on his journey and had made new, colorful clothes for him to wear. After all, he was representing the ranch, and they were proud of him. The five-peso piece was carefully placed in his pocket. He walked for a full day, except when he would jump on the back of a farmer's cart and ride. The first night he slept on the ground, for he didn't want to waste any money for a room in an inn. All this money was to buy the special present to take to the altar.

He walked a second day, and the second night he slept beneath a large tree. In the morning he awoke to see a beautiful white flower in the top of the tree. He climbed to pick the flower, but on his way down his foot slipped, and he fell through the limbs to the ground. The boy was shaken but unhurt, and the flower, which was still intact, would make the perfect decoration for his present.

Late in the afternoon of the third day of the boy's journey, he arrived in Mexico City. It was just as he had remembered it. The smells of bread and chocolate filled the streets, and the people were all dressed in bright colors. The boy went from shop to shop, looking for just the right present. He carried his flower carefully in his hand.

Then, in the shop of a woodcarver, he found what he wanted. It was a burrito—a tiny wooden burro carved from wood, with tiny cedar sticks bound to his back with leather strips. The boy asked its price, and the woman behind the counter told him five pesos. Filled with excitement he reached into his pocket for the money—*but it was gone.* He searched every pocket in his clothing, but the coin was nowhere to be found. Finally he left the shop without a present and sat in front of the church in which the service was to be held and cried.

"What a stupid boy I am," he thought. "The coin must have slipped out of my pocket when I fell from the tree. And now it is too late to go back to look for it. I have failed the old man and all the people on the ranch. And worst of all, I have no present for the Christ Child, except the flower," which by now was wilted and turning brown.

Soon people began to fill the church and the service began. The boy walked inside the large, dark interior lighted only by candles at the very front of the church. From his seat in the very back, he could see the priests in their bright vestments and hear the chanting of the service.

As the service ended the people began to walk up the aisle to take their gifts to the altar. The boy decided to walk at the end of the line and take the only gift he had—the wilted brown flower.

The boy covered the flower with his hand as he placed it among all the other beautiful presents in hopes that no one would see what an awful present he had brought. As he placed the flower down quickly and turned to go, he heard a gasp. He had been found out! Others had seen his pitiful gift. He turned back, to find that his brown, wilted flower had been replaced by a beautiful red flower with green leaves—*la flor de la noche buena.*

These are legends I traditionally tell at Christmas. Although they are not from the Bible, they come from the oral traditions of Europe and North America and express a love for the nativity. I especially like the fact that they include all of creation, plants and animals alike, in the celebration of the birth of Jesus.

These are well suited for fellowship gatherings, class parties, or family celebrations during the Christmas season. All ages can delight in their imaginative elaborations on the narratives of Jesus' birth.

Another way you might wish to use these stories is to weave them into a reading of the Christmas stories from the Gospels. Such a program of readings, stories, and songs could brighten even the darkest midwinter evening.

15

The Temple's True Foundation

Psalm 133
Two Brothers

> *Sometimes we Christians act as if we invented love. There are numerous stories that remind us that Jesus drew directly upon his (and thus our) Jewish tradition for the call to love that he lived out and preached. Love cannot be kept or owned but must be given away. Have you experienced such love? Is that the spot where you have built your temple?*

The Jewish people tell this story. Once there were two brothers who lived side by side on farms. One of the brothers was married and had children, while the other brother never married and lived alone. They cared for each other deeply.

One day the brother who lived by himself began to worry about his brother who had a family. He said to himself, "My brother has many mouths to feed and all the concerns that go with a family, and all I have to care for is myself. I certainly have more than enough for one. But I do not know if my brother would ever come to me for help."

So the solitary brother hit upon a plan to assist his brother without his knowing it. Every night he would carry a basketload of grain from his own barn to that belonging to his brother. His

85

brother would never notice one basket of grain more or less. In this way he could give to his brother without his ever knowing and feeling obligated to thank or repay him.

At about the same time the married brother had the thought, "Look how fortunate I am, with such a fine family to care for me now and in my old age. Yet my brother has no one but me. I have more than enough for me and my family. But I do not know if my brother would ever come to me for help."

So the married brother decided upon a way to help his brother without his knowing it. Every night he would carry one basketload of grain from his barn to the barn of his brother. He was sure his brother would never notice one basketload of grain more or less. In this way he could help his brother without his ever knowing and feeling obligated to thank or repay him.

After each brother had carried out his plan for several months, they both noticed that they never seemed to have fewer baskets of grain, though they carried one away each night. This just went to prove, each thought, that a basketload of grain more or less would never be noticed.

One night when the moon was full, each brother set out from his barn at exactly the same hour to make his nightly journey to the barn of the other brother. As they approached the boundary between their farms, each saw someone coming toward him in the distance. They met right on the boundary between their farms. When each recognized the other and they confessed to each other what they had been up to, they put down their baskets and laughed and embraced.

Such love is rare, the rabbis used to say, even among brothers. This is the reason that, in honor of the love the brothers showed for each other, Solomon built his temple on the spot where they met.

While this is usually viewed as a children's story and serves well in worship or the classroom, it could also be the perfect story for a homecoming celebration, a groundbreaking, or the dedication of a new building. This could be a particularly formative story for those who are beginning new churches.

16

Surprised by Faith

Luke 15:11-32
Monica and Her Son

We never truly know what fears keep others awake in the wee hours of the morning. Usually, though, those fears reflect love for the people for whose welfare they are concerned. Here is a story about a mother's love and fear for her son—and the rest is history.

Monica awoke from a terrifying dream. She had seen her son falling down a deep, dark hole. He was falling faster and faster, and though she called out to him, he could not seem to hear her. As he fell he was laughing the most horrible laugh, as if he was not afraid but was enjoying the fall. That was when Monica woke, with the sound of that laugh still ringing in her ears.

She walked to the window and looked out into the night. The sky had not yet begun to lighten with the coming sun. In the black sky the stars sparkled and the moon stood silent watch over the earth. Monica spoke to herself, to the night, to God: "If only he could get his life in order . . ." She had tried to talk to her son, but nothing seemed to help.

Monica was a Christian woman and had always hoped to be a good influence on her son. He was a bright and energetic boy, gifted in ways that would make him a great leader some day. But in his teens he went off to school and got mixed up with the wrong crowd. That was when his life went off track. He seemed to change entirely, going wild, doing things that Monica did not even want to imagine.

After a time she found out that he had fathered a child by a woman he seemed to have no interest in marrying. There was no talking to him at all by that time. She was left to her terrifying dreams with no one to tell her worst fears to except God and the night. She stood, numb all over, at the window, and the silence that surrounded her was like that of the tomb.

One day years later her son would come to his senses and turn his life around. He would dedicate his life to God and begin to use his gifts for the good of God's people. But on that lonely night Monica knew nothing of this future change. Her heart was breaking because she just knew that her son would never hear that her words were an expression of love rather than judgment.

After he did finally hear, Augustine of Hippo wrote about his life with brutal honesty in a book called *Confessions*. When he writes about his mother, Monica, he calls her "the voice of God."

Luke 12:32-34

Polycarp

What makes a person a hero? Is a hero someone who does not know fear, or someone who faces fear and overcomes it for a greater good? Polycarp is as unlikely a hero as you will ever meet. Is it possible that we unlikely people might find ourselves in circumstances that call on us to be heroic in faith?

Polycarp never intended to become a martyr. All in all, he had lived a fairly quiet life. Now he had come to a great old age and had become bishop of the church at Smyrna. He expected to live out his life in that same place in the same quiet way.

Then there came to the throne an emperor who hated Christians and wanted to destroy them. The emperor's soldiers went through town after town, gathering up Christians and forcing them to worship a statue of the emperor. Those who would not were killed.

When Polycarp heard that the soldiers were coming, he hid in a barn and advised all the other Christians to do the same. After all, he was no hero and had no intention of being a martyr. But it did not take the soldiers long to discover the aged bishop.

They brought him out of his hiding place along with all the other Christians they could find. Then they told Polycarp that he would have to worship a statue of the emperor and say that the emperor is lord.

"My Lord has been faithful to me all these years. How could I desert him now?" the aged bishop responded. "No, the emperor is not lord. Jesus Christ is Lord."

The soldiers took Polycarp away. He had never intended to become a martyr. He simply could not desert one who had been his faithful friend throughout his life.

The emperor took away Polycarp's life but he could not touch the friendship that allowed the old bishop to face death without fear.

I Corinthians 1:25-31

Genesius and God

No matter how well we think we understand baptism, God's act of bringing persons into the circle of friendship remains a mystery. Genesius, like Saul before him, is a most unusual candidate to become a friend of the friends of God. Perhaps this story serves as a reminder that it is God who calls persons into our circle.

Once there was a young man whose name was Genesius. He was an actor in the Roman theater and performed in the comedies that provided entertainment for the public. He and the troupe of players with which he worked specialized in creating humorous scenes that made fun of people or groups they thought were particularly foolish. They made fun of masters and slaves, of citizens and senators, of teachers and students.

But the groups at which they most enjoyed poking fun were religious. First, their teachers, preachers, and rituals were easy to spoof. Many almost seemed to be parodies of themselves. Second, the actors could count on the fact that most of the religious people they made light of would not be in the audience. Pious Jews, for example, would not be seen at the theater.

The group the company of players was working on at the time was a fairly new Jewish sect that had begun to include Gentiles as well. They were followers of a rabbi named Jesus and called themselves Christians. They claimed that when they ate bread and drank wine in their services, they were eating the body and drinking the blood of their founder. This sounded pretty ghoulish to the Roman audience, who would gasp in mock horror, then howl with laughter, when the actors brought out loaves of bread in the shape of hands and feet and began to munch on them.

Another ritual of the Christians, and a favorite of Genesius's, was called baptism. This was the way new members were initiated into the sect, after a long period of study. Genesius had a starring role in this skit, and the audiences loved him. It involved the cast walking in on either side of Genesius, all dressed in white and in a very solemn procession. Then at the very last moment, before the others were to walk Genesius into a fake Roman bath, he would raise his hand, grab his nose, and plunge into the water feet first. This always brought a laugh. Then the crowds really went wild when Genesius's head appeared above the surface spouting water like a fountain from his lips.

He became so popular that he was called by many Genesius

the Comedian. Then, during one performance, something strange happened. Genesius jumped into the water just as he had so many times before, but this time something was different. He didn't come to the surface quickly. At first he thought, "This is ridiculous—Roman baths are not deep." Then, as his lungs began to ache for breath, he thought for a moment that he was dying.

When he finally came to the surface, he did not spout water as always before. No, this time he stood and drank in the air as if he had risen from his grave. The crowd was not impressed. But Genesius was.

He went to the local community of Christians and told them what had happened. With no religious instruction and even without a priest or bishop present, he had taken part in a mock baptism done by a group of comedians, and something about him would never be the same. The Christians were not sure about his story. Actors were not allowed to be part of the community at the time. But the young man seemed to be sincere, and the community was not sure that God had not taken a hand in the whole business. So they allowed him to stay.

Later, during a period of severe persecution of the church, Genesius was given a chance to prove his sincerity. He was willing to die rather than deny the faith he had come to while intending to make fun of it.

Sometime later the church decided he would have a special place among those they remembered. To this day he is called Saint Genesius the Comedian.

Christian heroes are not always very heroic, at least not as we usually define that term. The women and men who have formed our faith across the centuries were flesh and blood, and had the same failings and strengths that we have.

I usually tell these stories as family stories, since these are some of our brothers and sisters from long ago. Polycarp, the bishop in hiding, Augustine, the wild and riotous youth,

91

Monica, the worried mother, and Genesius, cynical artist surprised by faith, are like those who make up our present-day families. These stories are not just for all of us, they are about all of us, too.

A hint: I often tell the story about Genesius at baptisms.

17

The Lives of Assorted Saints

Mark 9:40
Saint Patrick and Finn McCuhal

From Peter's first step into Cornelius's house, Christianity has struggled to be an inclusive faith. This story from the folk tradition gives not only a flavor of Celtic Christianity but also one more invitation to the church to meet the world with open arms.

During the days when Patrick was preaching and teaching all across Ireland, the people of that land became very fervent Christians. Once there was a group of men and women working in a field. When they stopped to rest, a young girl asked them to tell her the ancient tales of Ireland—the tales of Cucullain, Dierdre, and Finn McCuhal.

"Oh, no," the elders spoke up quickly. They had heard those same stories when they were young. But since they had become Christians, they believed that these tales were pagan. The only stories they were willing to tell were from the Bible. "We could not tell the tales of Cucullain, Dierdre, and Finn

McCuhal. Those are pagan myths. Why, those people didn't even exist."

No sooner had the words come out of their mouths than in the distance they heard the pounding of hoofbeats and saw a cloud of dust rising above the road that led to that field. Those who had heard the ancient tales as children knew immediately who was coming.

Sure enough, there soon appeared the roan steed of one of the people the elders had just now called fictitious. It was Finn McCuhal and his army, the Fianna. The elders quaked in their shoes, while the young girl looked on with excitement.

Just then from another direction came a group of monks, led by Patrick himself. "Now you'll see," the elders told the young girl; "Patrick will defeat this Finn and his whole army."

Finn with the Fianna and Patrick with the monks arrived at just about the same time. Steam rose from the nostrils of Finn's roan horse, so that it looked like smoke and the horse like a dragon. No sooner had they all arrived than Patrick approached the man on the horse.

"If I'm not mistaken, you're Finn McCuhal," said Patrick.

"That I am. Why is it you're wanting to know?" replied Finn.

To which Patrick laughed and said, "Come down off your horse and sit with us under the trees. Tell us the ancient tales of Ireland—the tales of Cucullain, Dierdre, and your own exploits."

So Finn climbed down and sat beneath the trees with his army, the monks, the elders, and the young girl. There he told the ancient tales of Ireland. And he listened as Patrick told the tales of Abraham and Sarah, Saul and David, Ruth and Naomi, and Jesus. And in that fashion they spent the afternoon, the young girl hearing more than she had dreamed of the stories she had asked for.

That is why they say that even today at the hearthsides of Ireland you will hear the stories of the Bible, but you will also hear the tales of Cucullain, and Dierdre, and Finn McCuhal.

Genesis 1:20-31
Saint Francis and the Creation

One of the few saints recognized by the Roman church, other churches, and outside the church altogether is Francis of Assisi. The simplicity of his chosen way of life has inspired renewal movements in Christianity ever since his life and death left a lasting aroma of holiness to drift down the halls of history. It is always easier to admire the saints than it is to imitate them.

In the city of Assisi there lived a young man whose name was Giovanni di Bernardone. His father was a well-to-do cloth merchant, which meant that Giovanni's youth was free from the drudgery of work. Everything he needed and much more was provided for him. He spent his time in the games and parties of the idle young in Assisi. He was so devoted to his fun that his friends laughingly called him "Francesco," or "Frenchy."

Along with the majority of the young men of his time, he entered the military and was soon involved in the fighting against Perugia. His family thought this time of military service would be good for him, would give him time to mature. He was taken as prisoner of war and returned to his family broken in body and spirit. The illness that had developed in prison lingered after his return to Assisi.

In the midst of his recovery, Francis vowed to live a life devoted to God. One way this new life took shape was in his desire to live in poverty, to give his belongings to the poor and live as they did. Francis's family and friends were startled by the new direction this young man's life had taken. He no longer entered into the games and parties that had occupied so many of his earlier days. He refused to spend the money his father made from the sale of cloth on these pastimes.

Instead, he took cloth from his father's storehouses and gave it to the poor for clothing. He spent the rest of his time

95

making mud brick and carrying stones to build fallen-down churches. His friends just ignored him, but his family was very worried. His father attempted to talk sense to his son, telling him that he could not just give away cloth to the poor. It was expensive cloth; the poor were not prepared to appreciate such rare and fine quality. He would give Francis the money he needed to have a good time with his friends, as he had in the old days before his illness. But Francis was not the same person he had been in the old days.

In desperation Francis's father asked the local priests and the bishop to talk to his boy. By this time Francis wore only a robe of rough brown cloth. It stood in stark contrast to the ornate grandeur of the bishop's vestments. The bishop told Francis on God's authority that he must not give away any more cloth to the poor.

"Did not our Lord tell the rich young ruler to take all he had and give it to the poor?" Francis questioned.

Unblinkingly, the bishop answered, "But what you have chosen to give away does not belong to you; it is your family's."

"Then the very cloth that hangs on my shoulders this very instant is my family's as well, I suppose?" The young man spoke in slow, measured phrases.

"Quite right." The bishop was pleased that Francis seemed to be coming around.

"Very well," Francis said as he began to undress, "would you kindly give this robe to my father and tell him that from now on I will be no one's child but God's, and I will have no family but God's creatures." Francis ended the conversation by walking away wearing not a single stitch.

While he worked, clothed again in a plain brown robe that had been given to him, moving stones and working mud into bricks so that a church, long dead, could be reborn, Francis felt the warmth of the sun. "Is not the sun my brother?" he thought. As he looked up at the night sky, he thought, "Is not the moon my sister?" As he and a few others who wanted to live for God would sit by the fire, Francis called the fire their brother and the earth their sister. The wind that patterned the grass on the hillside was brother, the water that fell from the heavens to gather into streams was sister.

For the rest of his life Francis never had to worry about having a family, for all creation was his family.

John 14:27
Lady Julian and Jesus

The gospel is a word of hope. The simplicity of Lady Julian's relationship with her friend, Jesus, and the word of hope he offers to the world through her may just be loud enough to drown out the shouts of hatred and the gunshots of war that fill our world.

Lady Julian of Norwich never made a lot of money. She never led armies or built cities. She was never elected to head a government, nor did she ever win a prize. She lived quietly as a sister in a Benedictine house in England.

She did write, however. Now, what she wrote never made the best seller list. She never had anything of hers made into a movie. No, she wrote books about what she saw and heard when she prayed.

When she was thirty years old, she became very ill. So ill, in fact, that she and others thought she would die. But she recovered and began to write about her experiences at prayer.

Jesus, she wrote, was her Friend, who showed her various scenes from his life and spoke to her about her own. Once when things looked very dark to Julian, her Friend spoke words of comfort that made her feel that no matter what she lived through, it would turn out well.

But the words were not for her life only. They were words for all situations and all times.

The voice of Jesus said to her, "All shall be well, and all shall be well, and all manner of thing shall be well."

No, Lady Julian was not rich or famous. But when things look dark for us and for our world, it is the word from her Friend (and ours), Jesus, that we long to hear and know in our hearts.

"All shall be well, and all shall be well, and all manner of thing shall be well."

Stories of the lives of saints are usually a free intermingling of historical events and persons with the spice of legend and imaginative remembering. Patrick, Francis, and Lady Julian are historical figures about whom little is known. But much of their spirit has been saved for us by the religious imagination.

I frequently tell the story of Patrick to begin a telling that will include stories from a number of traditions. If it was good enough for Patrick, it's good enough for me.

The Francis story might be included in a worship service in which the Prayer of Saint Francis is said, or at any gathering devoted to peace and reconciliation.

The story of Lady Julian is of a quiet and meditative nature. It could introduce a time of altar prayer in worship or in a camp setting, or begin a period of family prayer at home.

For other stories of this type, look in your library for stories of the saints.

18

A Story and a Teller

Matthew 5:43-48
The Angels, the Egyptians, and God

When Jesus told his disciples to love their enemies, he was not changing the rules. God's love, even for those we consider our enemies, is part of the witness of Jesus' Bible: the Torah, the Prophets, and the Writings. In the following story we are reminded that we are not the only ones who live by high ideals and standards.

The story is told that the angels in heaven were watching the Israelites as they crossed the sea to escape the Egyptian army. When the children of Israel made it safely to the other side into freedom, God heard a cheer go up from the heavenly host. God smiled that the people who had been slaves were on their way to a new land and life.

Then, as the armies of the Pharaoh prepared to cross between the walls of water, the heavenly company watched with intense interest. When they saw the water crashing in on the chariots and soldiers of Egypt, another even louder cheer arose. When God heard the second cheer, a shadow crossed the face of the Divine. God's voice called out, fearing already the cause of the second shout: "Why do you shout for joy again?"

"Your enemies, the Egyptians, have drowned in the crashing waters through which your children passed unharmed," came the answer from the angels.

"Then I want no cheering." God's voice was determined, even angry. "While my children called Israel have landed safely on freedom's banks, my children the Egyptians have drowned in the sea. I will tolerate no celebrations while any of my children die."

Psalm 149:1-4

The Rabbi and the Children

The storytelling tradition of the Hasidic Jews is having a profound influence on modern religious thought and expression. Through such writers as Martin Buber and Elie Wiesel, these stories and the culture from which they emerged are being shared with an audience that crosses religious and cultural boundaries. It is interesting to note that the subject of this story lived at about the same time as John Wesley.

Rabbi Israel ben Eliezer was well respected in his own community. He began a movement among his people that he hoped would give life back to a religion he thought was dead. The people who agreed with him were called the Hasidim, the faithful ones. They called their rabbi Baal Shem Tov, which means "keeper of the Good Name." It was said that only a few people in the world knew the secret name of God. They believed their rabbi was one of them.

The Baal Shem, as he was called, taught that to worship God was a joyful thing. So he and his followers would sing and dance as they worshiped. In addition, he told stories. The tales he spun were webs of enchantment that caught listeners up and transported them to far distant worlds. He never wrote his stories down, but after a time his students began to record them in writing so they would not be lost.

Stories were told about the Baal Shem, as well. He became a famous figure among the Hasidim. Those on the outside were not as kind. They would often make fun of the songs, dances, and stories of the Hasidim and their rabbi. When his students would try to tell of their wonderful teacher, those who opposed him would say, "Why, your rabbi is no teacher. He's nothing but a teller of stories to children." In that way they hoped to discredit him.

Centuries have passed, and the names of most of those who opposed the Baal Shem and his Hasidim have been long forgotten. But people around the world—Hasids and those who are not Hasids, Jewish folk and those who are not Jewish, religious folk and those who care little for religion—still listen to the stories told by or about Rabbi Israel ben Eliezer.

It seems that one could do worse than be a teller of stories to children.

The Jewish tradition of storytelling has exerted a profound influence in my life and my telling of stories. Of course, those wonderful stories from the Old Testament and the stories Jesus told were the beginning of my acquaintance with Jewish stories. But the influence did not stop there. Israel ben Eliezer and the other rabbis of the Hasidic movement have been my teachers right alongside those biblical storytellers. All have an uncanny ability to hold meaning and mystery together in tension, bringing us to the very edge of what words can say about God.

I include their stories in my preaching, teaching, and almost every setting in which I interact with people. Once, concerned that I was telling so many stories from a tradition other than the one I was born into, I asked a friend, a Jewish storyteller, if she was troubled by my telling the stories of her heritage. She said, "No, the stories belong to the world, to anyone who will hear them. They simply came to the world through us."

Be aware when telling a story from another tradition that it is important to learn as much as possible about that tradition and to tell the stories in a manner that will honor and enrich both the heritage of the story and all those who hear it.

IV

Friends from Many Places

The following stories are of two kinds. Some of them are about people I admire and consider friends, though I do not know them personally. The other stories are drawn from my own life experience and friends who have meant a great deal to me personally.

You will notice that my personal friends are referred to by their first names only (except for Señor Martinez, whom I never dreamed of calling by another name). Those friends whose lives I have only heard or read about are called by their full names.

You will probably know some or all of my friends whose lives are part of our public record, and the portions of their lives that you recall may be different from those I mention here. Each of us will recall a friend in a different way, remembering those things that are important to us.

You will probably not know any of my personal friends mentioned here. But I hope that the stories of their friendship toward me will spark your own memories of those persons who have served as true friends to you.

19

The Gifts of Friends

Isaiah 53:1-5
A Friend and a Cross

Stories from our own experience can provide a means of sharing our faith with others. This is a story about a gift of grace, a simple gift that meant more to me than the giver could know or I could say at the time. Have you ever received such a gift? Who has let you know that it is your scars that make you beautiful, like the servant in Isaiah?

It had been a tough year. In fact, there had been a number of tough years in a row. And now it was Advent again. I had tried to disguise my deepening depression with wisecracks and humorous stories. Christmas was on the way, but I was finding it difficult to keep up any kind of spirit at all.

Each Sunday evening in Advent, a special program was scheduled at the church. This particular evening we had gathered for a covered dish supper in the fellowship hall before the program, a series of readings from various stories about Christmas. I had eaten quickly and excused myself to go to the sanctuary and make sure the readers' stands were in place and the microphones were working.

Once alone in the half-dark sanctuary, I felt the relief

offered by the evening quiet. I simply sat for a time, basking in the shadows of the coming night. I knew others would be coming soon, so after a time I got up and began to make last-minute preparations for the readings. As I did this, one of the side doors of the sanctuary opened, and a head appeared around it.

"I thought you might be here," a voice spoke rapidly. "I don't want to disturb you. I know you're busy."

"It's all right. I'm just checking some last-minute details." The fact is, I was pleased to have my solitude interrupted by a friend. And Sydney was a friend. She was one of those persons who seem to travel through life a mile a minute but are never too busy to perform some act of kindness for someone who needs a smile or a word of encouragement.

Sydney handed me a small white box. "I have something for you. I made it, and thought of you so I brought it by. See you later." And she was gone as suddenly as she had appeared.

After the sanctuary door had thumped closed, I opened the box. Beneath a layer of cotton lay a small cross made of red stained glass. I knew that Sydney worked in stained glass and that she was getting quite a fine reputation as an artist. But I never imagined I would possess any work of her hands.

There were several other objects in the box with the cross. There were two cords with which one might wear the cross, one red and one black, and there was a handwritten note. I opened the note and read there the evidence that at least one of my parishioners and friends had seen through my charade of happiness. Apparently, the shadows that had passed through my heart had crossed my face as well.

Sydney told me she had seen a certain sadness on my face in recent weeks. While she did not know the reason, she wanted to share something with me that had given her happiness—her art. She ended the note with these words: "You will notice that there are marks that cross one side of the glass. These are not streaks; they are natural in stained glass. We call them scars. They are there to remind you that it is our scars that make us beautiful."

The people began coming into the sanctuary for the evening

readings. That night Sydney smiled up at me from the crowd. After the program she was gone too quickly for me to thank her.

The next Sunday I wore the cross. I have it to this day and wear it often, always scar-side out.

John 15:13
Maximilian and His Fellow Prisoner

No greater love can anyone show than to give up life for a friend. This is God's love, Jesus' love, tough love. This love is demanding on the lover and the beloved. Yet if God so loved the world, can we love it and its inhabitants any less?

Maximilian Kolbe was a Catholic priest from Poland who lived as a part of the largest community of Franciscan priests and brothers in the world. He and the others in his community published magazines and prepared radio broadcasts to share their understanding of faith with others. When the Nazi army arrested a number of religious leaders, Kolbe was among them.

The priest found himself in Auschwitz with hundreds of other prisoners, both Jewish and Christian. Everyone's head was shaved and all were dressed in prison uniforms. Kolbe and the other prisoners who were able were forced to perform hard labor. Those too weak to work were killed or left to die.

In the face of such a cruel situation, Kolbe became a chaplain to the other prisoners, listening to their fears and hurts as the days and weeks passed.

One day the guards entered the section of the camp where Kolbe was kept and announced that a prisoner was missing. They assumed he had escaped. (In fact, he had not.) To keep others from attempting the same thing, they chose at random ten from among those still there, for execution. Kolbe knew that one of the prisoners chosen had a wife and children who were not in the camps. Before the guards could leave with the ten, Kolbe spoke up: "Take me instead of him." The priest pointed to the husband and father.

The guards were astounded that this man would willingly offer his own life for another. They thought he must be crazy. He simply told them he was a priest, with no wife or children to return to someday. So the guards took Kolbe instead of the other man, to be locked in a cell with the other nine. The ten were then left to die of hunger and thirst.

Maximilian Kolbe died in Auschwitz in 1941, while the husband and father whose place he took in the death line lived to survive the camp and the war. Forty-one years later in Rome, when Pope John Paul II declared Maximilian Kolbe a saint, there was a very interested guest watching: the man who had lived because the priest had chosen to take his place. He was at that time eighty-one years old.

Psalm 150
Charlie and His Music

Charlie was one of the "characters" I came to know in my youth. While these people are not necessarily good role models, they add color and texture to life, without which it would be as bland as Cream of Wheat. Many of the characters of the Bible are not especially good role models either. But who are we to say that their fractured lives do not sing God's praises louder than our pious words?

Charlie always seemed to come into my life in the fall, just about the time that school started. I would look up one hot late August morning to see him walking up Preacher's Mill Road toward the house. The house was the home my Uncle Lee and Aunt Ann rented. We lived across the road from them in a trailer. Uncle Lee was my father's brother. His wife, Aunt Ann, was Charlie's sister.

Charlie was what people in those days called a "carny,"

meaning he worked for one of the carnival companies that came to small towns across the country once a year to provide the rides and booths for the county fair. Quite a few folks didn't think too highly of Charlie's way of life. But to me as a child he was the most remarkable man I had ever met.

As a young man Charlie had been a musician in a bluegrass band in North Carolina. Aunt Ann had a framed photograph of the group in her bedroom. There was Charlie, twenty-five years younger, holding his fiddle and wearing the thin mustache he still wore.

Charlie no longer played with bands, and the mustache that once had been black was gray. He told me he had given up playing the fiddle because of a "shrunken" little finger. Sure enough, it was smaller than the other one and was drawn toward the middle of his hand. So I never heard him play the fiddle, but from time to time I would talk him into playing a tune on the guitar.

I would bring my guitar across the road to Aunt Ann's, and Charlie would ask to hear the three chords I knew at the time. He always had praise for anything I could produce that bore the slightest resemblance to a song. Then it was his turn.

Each time he played the same tune. I assume that he knew others, but I never heard evidence of it. The tune was called "The Spanish Fandango." There were no words to it, as far as I knew. Charlie watched his hands as he played, his fingers moving slowly and painfully up and down the neck of the guitar. In my eyes, I might as well have been sitting in a master class with André Segovia.

As amazing as his music were Charlie's stories. During summers he had traveled all across the country with several of the better-known carnivals. In wintertime he lived in Florida, working with a show that had a semipermanent home there. He seemed to have a story from every place he visited. He told of visits to Mexico and Cuba and even some places I had never heard of in geography class.

After a night or two Charlie would be on his way, gone for another year. After a time my family moved to a different road, across the river from my uncle and aunt. I did not see Charlie for a number of years, until one day in college, when I happened to be passing through the bus station in Nashville. After I checked in at the window I began to look for a seat. And there, sitting by the window, was Charlie. I sat next to him, and we tried to catch up on the lost years. He had stopped traveling with the shows and was living in a cheap hotel in Nashville. I told him I would try to get by to see him. My bus came, and we said good-bye. I neither saw nor heard from Charlie again.

Sometimes when the world seems too ordinary, too everyday, I think of Charlie, of his stories and songs. Then somewhere in the distances of memory I can hear, being slowly and painfully played, "The Spanish Fandango."

Matthew 20:25-26
Kagawa

The most simple act of friendship reveals God. Our sisters and brothers from the Asian countries have much to teach the rest of us about the importance of simple acts. In oriental art a few simple brush strokes create an entire landscape. In haiku a few simple words create a world of feeling and experience. In this story a simple act on the part of one person becomes a way of expressing the love of God through even the most ordinary of daily duties.

Toyohiko Kagawa was a well-known Japanese pastor and poet. During the years before World War II, his name became a household word in many parts of the world, primarily because of his work with the poor in his country. Born into a Buddhist family, Kagawa became a Christian as a young person. He was educated in Japan and in the United States. From very early in his ministry he felt a love for and an identity with the poor. He moved into the slums of Kobe where he helped to provide bread and clothing for the people. This help was linked in Kagawa's life with prayer and preaching and the writing of poems.

110

Because of his dedication to the people among whom he lived and his writings that were published around the world, Kagawa was frequently invited to speak to and meet with groups of Christians in various parts of the globe. He combined a strong and lively faith with a desire to live among and share the joys and pains of the least of God's people. He even took part in a strike by the workers of Kobe that helped to begin the labor movement in Japan. Kagawa's faith touched all parts of his life and the lives of those with whom he shared the world.

During his travels this pastor/poet often met and shared the speakers' platform with many of the most famous and influential people in the Christian faith. This story is told of one of those meetings:

During a break in this particular meeting Kagawa and a number of the dignitaries at a global meeting of Christians stopped by a restroom. On their way out the others were talking with their Japanese colleague when they noticed that he was no longer with them. When they returned to the restroom, they found him picking up the towels that they had carelessly thrown at the wastebasket and missed, leaving them on the floor. When he had finished, he joined his companions without a word. He didn't need to say anything. A simple act of consideration spoke volumes.

During World War II Kagawa was imprisoned by his government. After the war some of his friends encouraged him to enter politics, but he was not interested. He simply continued to serve and preach and write as he had before.

In our time Toyohiko Kagawa is not a household word; he is no longer famous. Yet his greatness, at least as Jesus defined the word, lives on.

You have probably noticed that among these stories of friends from recent times are those about people I have known personally and those about people I know only through the stories told about them by others. But I consider all of these people friends of mine (and friends of God) because of the influence of their stories on my life, whether I know them personally or not. Simply hearing and telling about them helps me to know what it means to be a friend to God and others.

I hope that some of these stories have sent you spinning back into your own memory, recalling friends you have known or whose stories you have heard in the past. You may choose to tell one of the stories printed here, alongside a reading of the Scripture passage listed at the top of the page, as a brief devotional at a meeting, during a retreat or class, or simply during a time of family or personal devotions. But I trust the process will not stop there. I urge you to use these as models for telling stories from your own life, from memories of friends you have known in the flesh, and from the lives of friends who have taken on flesh for you in stories.

20

Friends as Teachers

Leviticus 19:33-34
Martin and Ramon

Have you ever felt like an outsider, excluded because of the way you talk or look or think? The stories of the Bible are full of outsiders, such as Ruth and Cornelius, who are welcomed into the circle of the friends of the friends of God. Here is a story about two childhood friends, rejected by other children, who continue to live in the circle of friends I carry with me in memory. Whenever an outsider is welcomed in, be sure that the reign of God cannot be far away.

The playground was awash with color. The clothing of the children as they ran in patterns defined by their games created a shifting tapestry across the sandy earth, worn clean of grass. I stood to the side and watched, feeling very much the outsider. My parents had brought me from Tennessee to the desert of southern Arizona for my health. My father had changed jobs so that we might live in this warm climate near the border with Mexico.

Even the faces of the children showed differences I had not known in school before. They were black and brown and white, some of the eyes were shaped differently from mine, and their accents sounded foreign to my ears.

Among the faces, two stood out because they too seemed to be left out of the play. A child from the larger group called to them, "Come on. You can play—but you have to be the Indians." Then there was laughter. "You sure couldn't be the cowboys," the voice added. The two youngsters standing alone lowered their heads so that all I could see was the part that ran right down the middle of their straight black hair.

I learned that these were two brothers who had been "adopted" from a tribe that lived near the Grand Canyon by one of the teachers at the school. They were taken from their home so that they might be educated in "the larger world." Their first names were Martin and Ramon. Only their faces and their last name identified them as Native Americans.

As the year passed we became friends, the two brothers and I. Even though I "talked funny," being from the South, I was still better accepted by the other children than my new friends. I found this hard to understand. Martin and Ramon were shy and considerably nicer and better behaved than most of our schoolmates. Although the brothers were quiet, when they did speak what they said was usually worth listening to. They often spoke of home. I do not remember much of what they told me, but I vividly recall their faces, which showed so little of their feelings, and the quiet way they spoke.

When school started the following year, my new friends were gone, along with the teacher who had brought them there. The year following that, my health having improved, my family returned to Tennessee. I have not seen Martin or Ramon since.

I do not know if their experience of "the larger world" contributed anything to their lives but the memory of the twisted laughter and harsh voices of the children of that world. But they gave me something that is almost beyond the power of words to describe. Perhaps that is the reason I carried their school photographs, stained from years of being carried in a brown leather wallet, long past my college days. Or perhaps that is why, in the quiet of some evenings, I can still hear their voices speaking words that, if only I could make them out, I would cherish for their wisdom and compassion.

John 14:1-3
Dharma

Sometimes it is tempting to reject the wisdom that comes from religious traditions other than our own. Yet many of the stories that are part of our Scriptures we share in other versions with other religions. The following story, told to me by a friend, helps to remind me that I do not hold the reservation book to the many rooms that God has prepared for those who are God's friends across the world.

My friend Dharma was born in Sri Lanka and served churches there before coming to this country. Though we first met in an official capacity as persons related to the same agency, very soon that official relationship turned into friendship. As I have talked with him, listened to some of his life experiences, and stayed in his home, I have come to respect Dharma's ability to appreciate and enter into the lives of those whose religious backgrounds are different from his own. His choice to bring his family to a vastly different setting to live and work is only one example of the risk involved in stepping across cultural boundaries.

As we visited together one day, he told me of an aspect of preaching common in Sri Lanka, which opened a doorway for me into understanding his caring approach to persons of different cultural backgrounds. Dharma mentioned that in his home country it was not uncommon for Christian preachers to include Hindu and Buddhist stories in their sermons. One reason they did this, he explained, was that there were often Buddhists and Hindus in the congregation, and the preacher did not wish to exclude them. In addition, there was great wisdom to be found in their stories.

This is a Buddhist story he told me. Once a woman came to the Buddha terribly upset because her child had died. She came with many questions: Why had this happened to her child? Why had death been so cruel to her when others lived to a ripe old age? Why could she not be consoled?

The Buddha sat and listened in silence. When the woman had finished her questioning, the Buddha spoke to her. "I will not answer your question now. But if you return bringing with you a mustard seed from a family that has not been touched by death, I will tell you anything you wish to know." The woman went on her way and did not return.

Through the stories of others, we begin to get a glimpse of their world. Perhaps true compassion comes from our attempts, however slight, to include others in our world and to glimpse the world through their eyes.

Psalm 8
Martin

In a speech to a group of teachers, Martin Buber once said that if he ever met the great Christian theologian Karl Barth, there was only one thing this bearded Jewish scholar would like to teach him. Buber wanted to teach him to dance the ecstatic dances of the Hasidic Jews. You can imagine the gleam in the aged scholar's eye as he said that.

Martin Buber knew about friendship. In fact, friendship was the way he talked about all our relationships with each other and with God.

Buber grew up in a religious home, in the household of his grandfather, a rabbi and a scholar. Very early Martin was recognized as a child who had a profound appreciation for both study and prayer. As a young man he attended the university and became active in politics. He was involved in the dreams of a Jewish homeland in Israel.

116

Then, in his late twenties, he changed directions in his life. While he continued to support efforts for a homeland, he ceased his political and editorial activities in order to study his own religious tradition. The young man began to read everything he could find of the writings and history of Hasidic Judaism, a renewal movement in Eastern Europe that began about the same time as the Methodist movement in England. For five years he studied the stories by and about the Hasidim, "the faithful ones."

The Hasidim believed that we know God not through learning or beliefs but through a direct encounter. Its founder, Israel ben Eliezer, was known as a teller of stories, and the Hasidim included storytelling and ecstatic dancing as part of their devotion to God. This emphasis on encountering God with delight and wonder left its mark on Buber.

When he was forty-five, a professor, writer, and editor, he published a book called *I and Thou*. In it Buber described two ways of relating to the world, other people, and God. Most of the time we treat others as if they were "Its," the way science looks at the elements of an experiment. It is only when we begin to view people with empathy that they become for us "Thous." We attempt to see the world through the experience of other persons, to respect them as unique human beings. Perhaps there is no better definition of a true friendship than to call it an I-Thou relationship.

According to Buber we can only come to know God as a Thou. Our knowledge of God is not simply learning facts about our faith, its history, or its beliefs, though these may help us understand our religious tradition. To know God is to enter into a friendship, an I-Thou relationship with God. Martin Buber gave us words to talk about our friendship with God.

Respect for persons of other cultural and faith traditions is deepened and increased by hearing their stories. The story of my two Native American schoolfriends might be told to help prepare children or youth for incorporating persons with different languages or cultures into the church or their class. The story from the Buddhist tradition that my friend

117

Dharma told me could be included as a part of a funeral meditation or when there has been a sudden death that affects the entire community.

Martin Buber's story, which expresses some of the same values as the previous two, is clearly for adults, especially those who value intellectual achievement. Buber's scholarship brought him to story, and story brought him to his important insight into our relationships to God and others as "Thous" rather than "Its." This story would fit in a campus ministry setting, even with professors, or would help set the stage for Christian-Jewish dialogue.

No matter what the setting or to whom you tell a story, its power to touch the heart as well as the mind comes not from the quality of the telling alone. The story's ability to move people depends heavily on how well it fits the occasion and the audience who will hear it.

Esther 9:26-28
Lynn

Did you ever think of a story having a tune? If you had to name the tune of the story of your life, what would it be? Perhaps the greatest gift another person can give us is to help us discover the tunes that carry our stories of faith like a melody on a distant breeze.

Lynn is a rabbi and a storyteller. She was the first woman rabbi I had met, and clearly the first woman rabbi–storyteller with whom I had come into contact. We worked together for several summers, leading workshops on storytelling.

I had grown up with the story traditions of the mountains of southern Appalachia, which included family stories, tall tales, ghost stories, Jack tales, and even Bible stories. Lynn had matured in a different tradition, one that included the humorous stories of Chelm, Hasidic tales, teaching stories of the rabbis, and the Bible too.

Over the years I had grown to have a particular affection for the stories of the Jewish tradition. The stories of the rabbis held mystery in tension with meaning and so taught better than they knew. The tales of the Hasidim placed the events of life in a larger perspective, helping me to remember what was really important. The stories recounted about the foolish people of Chelm reminded me of how the humor of my own tradition also allowed us to laugh at ourselves.

But the Bible stories! I had never heard anyone tell stories from Scripture the way Lynn told them. In the first place, she chanted them. That's right, she chanted the entire story, repeating the same pattern of notes throughout. And her chanted narratives held me entranced, carried along on waves of words and music.

Second, she was able to weave into familiar biblical narratives events and reflections that were unfamiliar to me, coming from the ongoing oral traditions of the Jewish people. She told me of Lilith, the woman who preceded Eve, for example. As she drew on the different versions of stories and on commentaries about them, I felt as if I were in the presence of something living and growing, rather than a faceless text that had been fixed centuries ago.

One evening Lynn told us the story of Hadassah (we know her as Esther). Her telling lasted half an hour, I suppose, though to tell you the truth I lost track of the time. At the end, when Esther saved her people from the plots of the evil Haman, there was that sense of relief one experiences when things finally turn out right.

As she ended the story, Lynn immediately began a prayer. The prayer was a plea that the children of Israel and the children of Ishmael learn to live in peace and mutual respect. I found myself wiping away tears. It wasn't a sad experience at all, but it was a moving one—it moved me beyond thinking that just because my people had been saved, the story was finished. For Lynn the story would not be finished until all people could live together in peace.

It took me a year to finally tell my friend that I wanted to be able to chant the stories of the Bible with the same kind of power she revealed in that telling. Her only reply was "You will find your own tune in which to tell them. My tune is for me, but you will discover the one that is for you."

Luke 17:5-10
Mary

"It can't be done." "One person won't make any difference." These phrases were not in the vocabulary of Mary McLeod Bethune. If she heard them, she ignored them and did what needed to be done—and made a difference.

If you were going to start a school, you would certainly want to begin with more than $1.50. And if you were raising money to keep the school going, you would probably not choose to raise funds by baking pies and selling them. But that is what Mary McLeod Bethune did to begin a school for black students that has become in our time Bethune-Cookman College.

Of course, the school did not begin as a college: It started by teaching the basic skills of learning. And Mary McLeod Bethune did not begin as a teacher. She was the youngest of seventeen children born to a family of slaves on the plantation of a family named McLeod. When she was nine years old, she still could not read or write.

Through the support of persons of various denominations, Mary was able to go to school, and finally to begin her own school. She began it with $1.50, a plan to sell home-baked pies, a desire to educate children, and five students. Later she would become president of Bethune-Cookman College and a friend to students, alumni, and national leaders, even presidents.

Shortly before her death, she wrote what she hoped would be her legacy to the world. She said, "I leave you love." A friend could not ask for more.

Luke 6:20-36
Mother Teresa

"Yes, but we can't all be Mother Teresa." Have you said that? I have. Do you suppose she said it before God called her to be more than she ever imagined she could be? Isn't the danger of becoming a friend of God that we might be called to such a radical faith as the one expressed in the Beatitudes?

She should have been content to teach the students at Saint Mary's High School in Calcutta. After all, that was what she had spent her life training to become—a teaching sister. From the time of her childhood in Yugoslavia through her training in Ireland, she wanted to be a Sister of Loreto. Following this calling had brought her to Calcutta in the first place.

Day after day, she stepped over or around people who had no place to live but the streets of Calcutta. Many of them were ill, some were dying with no place to go. One day, at the age of thirty-six, she asked her superiors for permission to end her teaching and to move, all alone, to one of the poorer sections of the city. She was given that permission, which would set her life on a new course that she could not even imagine.

Her calling, as she understood it, was to minister to the poorest of the poor. She wanted to provide a place for people to come or be brought to die, so that their lives would not have to end alone on the street. She wanted them to know that someone cared, that they had a friend.

She accepted Hindus, Buddhists, Muslims, and Christians without asking what religion they belonged to. Instead, she said that in each face she saw the face of Christ, and that as she

121

ministered to each dying person, she was doing the same for Christ.

Soon others joined her in Calcutta, and other houses were opened in cities across the world. She would be asked to speak to important gatherings and to accept degrees from major universities. She would be awarded the Nobel Prize and meet the pope.

Yet all these honors pale before this small woman dressed in a white sari with a blue cross and blue trim. It was her friends whose bodies she washed and whose spirits she lifted who were really important. The honor was in serving them and thus in serving her Lord.

The new direction her life took over forty years ago would affect not only her but the lives of those whom she serves, those who work with her, and those of us for whom her name, Mother Teresa, has become synonymous with friendship and compassion.

I Corinthians 12:4-11
Señor Martinez

Do you see yourself as gifted? To listen to the way we talk, you would think that only a few people are gifted with special abilities. But Saint Paul assumed that every member of the Body was gifted; the gifts were just different, that's all. How would our life together be different if we saw each person and activity as God's gift to our world community?

Señor Martinez was doing what the great Saint Francis of Assisi did; he was rebuilding God's church. At least he was rebuilding one of them. The Church of Santa Rosa de Lima near his home in Abique, New Mexico, had been abandoned years before. Built originally of adobe, the wind and weather had taken their toll, so that not a single one of its four walls stood complete.

So Señor Martinez, along with several young helpers, took it upon himself to rebuild the historic church, using the same mud from which the bricks had been formed when the walls were first raised. The dirt had to be dug from the mounds that encircled what was left of the original building.

It was almost by chance that two friends and I joined him in this project. We had been driving by and had simply stopped to ask what was happening. We got more than we bargained for. We heard a history of the church, a description of the present project, and got a job. Before we had been there half an hour, I was mixing straw into mud under the watchful eye of Señor Martinez.

We were making mud bricks in much the same way the Israelites had made them to build Pharaoh's royal cities, except that we were allowed as much straw as we needed, and Señor Martinez was not a harsh taskmaster.

One morning as we worked, our master brickmaker asked if we would honor him by coming to his home for a meal at noon. Of course, we were delighted to have been invited and accepted without hesitation. A little after midday, we drove up the long hill from the main road into Abique.

At the home of Señor Martinez, we were treated to a more than ample meal of beef, rice, and beans, along with the best sopapillas I have ever tasted, fried in a black cast-iron skillet. After the meal we walked farther up the hill behind the house to the home of Señor Martinez's mother. She spoke no English, and our Spanish left a lot to be desired. But when she showed us the brightly colored spreads she made by hand, we needed no translator. Her handiwork spoke for itself, beyond the barriers of language.

When the summer was over, the church had not been restored. In fact, I do not believe it has been completely rebuilt to this day. But as I remember Señor Martinez and his family, the care he took teaching us to make adobe and the respect in which he held that fallen-down building, I wonder if we were not building a different kind of church. Perhaps it is the kind not built with hands making bricks and mortar. Rather, this church is made as hands join other hands across all barriers of place and time.

I Thessalonians 5:16-18
Thomas

"Pray constantly." How in the world can anyone do that? Sure, if you go off to a monastery or live all alone, but even then you have to sleep. What might it mean in your life to let your work, your attitude, your very breath be your prayer?

Thomas Merton was full of surprises. He began as a writer. He and other students at Columbia University with literary interests would gather to talk about their writing projects. Under the tutelage of one of his professors, Mark Van Doren, the young Merton sharpened his skills in poetry and prose.

Then, over a period of several years, he began to take a more personal interest in religion. Finally, he surprised his acquaintances by becoming a monk. Not just any monk, mind you, but a Trappist. These monks take a vow of silence, a very strange course for a young writer.

But it was only after he entered the monastery that Merton began to publish the books for which he would be remembered. Perhaps the best known of his early works is *The Seven Storey Mountain*, the autobiography that tells of his life's journey to the monastery.

Much to his and everyone else's surprise, it was after Merton left the world that he became famous around the world. He kept in touch with the events taking place outside the walls of his community. For a monk vowed to silence, he was outspoken in support of civil rights and in opposition to the war in Vietnam. Many of his earlier fans were surprised and angered by his opinions on such worldly issues. After all, he was supposed to devote his time to prayer, not to meddling in the affairs of the world.

Yet it was his praying that made him care so deeply about the world and those who populate it. And it was his praying that led him to look to the East for kindred spirits. While he was perhaps the best-known Christian monk in the West, Merton began to study the spiritual traditions of Buddhism and Taoism. It seems that Merton could continue to surprise those who thought they had him figured out.

So through a life of poetry and prayer, silence and speaking out through his writing, and through taking part in the great spiritual traditions of the world, Thomas Merton came to maturity.

Then, just as we thought we would have years more to watch his changes and benefit from his wisdom, it seems there was another surprise in store for us all. On his first extended visit away from his community, he traveled to Bangkok for a meeting of monks from East and West. One night during this trip, he reached to turn on an electric fan in his room and was accidentally electrocuted.

Though Merton chose to live in a monastery, he remained a friend to the world. He was a friend to the brothers with whom he lived and to his readers, who could hardly keep up with the journey his writings recorded. He was a friend to those who were cut off from the good things that make life sweet and who were denied their rights as human beings. He was a friend to those who sought the way to God or truth or wholeness by a different path.

He was a friend always full of surprises.

John 15:15
You

God has called us friends, and a friend's story is important. All these stories have been intended to prime the pump, to get your memory and imagination transporting you down roads you never thought you would see, or see again. You are a friend of God, and a friend of the friends of God. Your stories are important.

Now it is the time to tell your story. You have favorite friends from the Bible, from the history and legends of the church, and from books about people you have admired. Perhaps the finest gifts you can give a friend, beyond your actual friendship, are stories of people you have come to love and respect.

Now that you have heard about a few of my favorites, it is time for you to choose your own. The stories you have read here represent only a very few of the multitude of the friends of God who can become your friends as well.

That is why the last story of this book is not my story, it is your story. Perhaps telling it will mark the beginning of a lifetime of telling the stories of those persons who accompany you along your journey of faith. No two people will choose the same stories, just as no two people will have exactly the same set of friends.

If you haven't begun already, now is the time for you to begin to gather your own collection of "friends for life."

Scripture Index

Scripture Index